A Dog on His Own

MARY JANE AUCH

Holiday House / New York

Library of Congress Cataloging-in-Publication Data
Auch, Mary Jane.
A dog on his own / by Mary Jane Auch. — 1st ed.
p. cm.
Summary: After a daring escape from the animal shelter, Pearl, Peppy, and
K-10—since he is one step above all the other canines—explore the outside
world while moving from one adventure to another.
ISBN 978-0-8234-2088-9 (hardcover)
[1. Dogs—Fiction. 2. Friendship—Fiction. 3. Homelessness—Fiction.
4. Adventure and adventurers—Fiction.] I. Title.
PZ7.A898Do 2008
[Fic]—dc22
2008015963

ISBN 978-0-8234-2243-2 (pbk.)

For all of the wonderful dogs
who have found their forever home
with our family over the years—
Kaiser, Gretchen, Kaiser the Second,
Fritz, Obie, Rudy, Sophie, and Zeke.

And special thanks
to the canine members
of my critique group, whose opinions
were invaluable for this book—
Josie DeFelice, Willis Brewster,
and Sadie Pulver.

Chapter

There's something funny about that white car. It went by me a few minutes ago, going in the opposite direction. Then it turned around in a driveway, and now it's coming back, slow and easy. This is where being able to read would come in handy, because there are big blue letters on the door.

The car stops, and two guys get out—a young one and an older fat one. They're not paying any attention to me, but something tells me I should pay attention to them. They're coming my way, crossing the street but not looking at me. I duck behind a bush and sniff the air. The younger one has that scent that people get when they're gearing up to do something hard or exciting, like going on a journey or running a race. My boy, Noah, used to smell a little bit like that on his first day of school every year.

I'm ducking down so I can see their feet. Okay, it was a false alarm. They're going right past me. But, wait! I'm getting another scent—a mixture of dogs, cats, urine, and disinfectant—the smell of an animal shelter! I gotta get out of here, fast! I only see one pair of feet now. Just as I'm turning, the fat guy comes up behind me. I scoot between his legs, knocking him off balance, then run around the back of a house.

"Watch out, he's getting away! He ran into the backyard."

Good, there's no fence—just a bunch of yards connected to each other. I take long strides and move like the wind. Fat Guy chases me behind the first few garages, then drops back. He's panting like an old bulldog. I keep running. I'm too fast and too smart to get caught. That's why my mom named me K-10, because I'm one step above the other dogs.

Woo-hoo!

I'm catching a whiff of something good now. Meat! I'm starving. Haven't eaten in a couple of days. Ah, I'm on the scent now. Must be just around the corner of this hedge. Yep, there it is—a big hunk of beef. Why would anybody leave that out here on the ground? Can't wait to sink my teeth into—"Hey! Hey hey hey hey hey hey HEY!" I bark.

A loop of rope drops over my head. Fat Guy from the shelter has it on the end of a long stick. Now he's pulling the cord snug around my neck. I roll and squirm and bite at the stick, but I can't get loose.

"Calm down, buddy," Fat Guy says as he eases me down the driveway.

"Calm down! Calm down? Let's see how calm you'd be with a noose around your neck, Fatso."

Young Guy is standing by their car. No wonder they got here so fast. They drove! That's not fair. They should give a dog a fighting chance. And since when did the shelter guys go around in a car, anyway? Last time I was caught, the guys were in a big truck with a picture of a dog on the side, to give us poor canines a clue. Unfair again!

Young Guy opens the back of the car, and

there's a big open cage inside. Before I know what's happening, they wrestle me into it, shut the door, and we drive off.

My heart is pounding fast. You never know what to expect at a shelter or pound. Sometimes the people are real nice and will keep a dog around until someone wants to adopt him. Other places aren't so nice, and if a dog doesn't find a family right away, they . . . well, I'm not going to think about that.

This is my . . . let's see, my fourth, fifth . . . no, my sixth time going to a shelter. Wow, I never stopped to count that up before. When I get out of here, I'm going to be a lot more careful.

We must be pulling up to the shelter now. Young Guy puts a collar and leash on me, and the two of them take me inside. I've never seen this place before. The lady at the desk yawns. She has that scent that people get when they're bored. "What's the story with this one?"

"No story," Fat Guy says. "No collar, no tags. Just another stray."

"I'm not a stray, I'm a free and independent dog," I bark, but they don't understand me.

The woman writes something on a piece of paper, then takes me into a kennel, where every dog starts barking at once. She closes me in a cage, then comes back with food and water. "Here's a nice meal for you, boy," she says. "You look like you haven't been eating too regular lately." She scratches me behind my ears before she closes my cage again. Looks like this may be a good place, but you can never tell. Could be just one nice lady in a bad shelter.

Somebody calls, "Hey, new guy. What's your name?"

I don't answer. I'm going to keep quiet tonight until I see what's what. Each one of these joints is a little different. Have to play it slow at first—feel out the situation. There are a few more shout-outs, but the commotion dies down when they all get the picture that I'm not talking.

The chow isn't anything special, but I've had worse. I polish it off, then settle in on my cot. I can sleep anywhere and eat anything. I'm lucky that way. My mom always told me it doesn't pay to be fussy, because you never know where you're going to end up. I bet she never pictured me in a place like this. Or maybe she did.

The only good thing about being in a cage is that you don't have to keep one eye open in case some other animal is sneaking up on you while you're sleeping. I'll catch up on my rest tonight. I'll probably be adopted tomorrow. Maybe I'll get a good home this time, not that it matters. I've had it with humans.

I only stayed a couple of days with the last guy. He seemed nice enough, but most humans do at first. Even if they start out by playing with you, taking you for long walks, and telling you what a good boy you are, pretty soon they start slacking off. Next thing you know, all you get is food in the dish, a pat on the head, and a quick stop outside, where they keep yelling, "Hurry up, do your business." They don't understand that a dog has to find the exact right spot, and it takes a lot of sniffing and circling to get there. And don't think I haven't noticed how long some people can squat on that pot in the bathroom to do *their* business. I had one owner who used to read the whole newspaper sitting in there—every day!

Anyway, this last owner, who called me Harley—I don't remember his name—he was still in the long-walks-and-playing stage, but I decided not to wait around for things to go bad. I slipped my collar and ran. So I'll play the "please take me home with you" game tomorrow, but it's only my ticket out of here. Nothing more.

I'm beat. At least it'll be good to have a few squares and a warm place to sleep tonight. Somebody's snoring down the hall. I start breathing in his rhythm, and pretty soon I'm heading for dreamland. Works every time.

I wake up the next morning when a guy comes in with food, and the others raise a ruckus all over again. Nobody's shouting for me, though. All anybody cares about is the food.

Before I get a chance to finish eating, the guy comes back. "Bath time, sport. You smell like a sewer."

He lifts me into a big sink and squirts that awful vermin-killing soap all over my fur. Man, that stuff reeks. Makes my eyes water. Never could understand why people love that fake perfume stuff, but when you smell like a natural dog, they think you stink.

The guy rinses off the soap with cold water from a hose. Sheesh! They never heard of hot water? He takes me into another room, and things start looking up. There's a beautiful girl smiling at me. "Well, aren't you a cute one?" I tilt my head and raise my right ear, just to show her I can be even cuter if I try. She laughs. Humans love that move—especially girls.

The girl puts me up on a table and starts drying me off with a big towel. Then she begins working on me with a brush and a hair dryer. Finally, I'm warming up. Being brushed makes me relax and start to daydream.

"You must have some golden retriever in you," Amy says.

She's right about that. I'm half golden. I was born on a farm and lived there with Mom and my brothers and sisters. Then one day a nice couple adopted me and called me Butterscotch. I don't remember their names. It was a good place to live at first, until they starting leaving me alone all day long. Pretty soon they stopped liking me and took me back to the farm.

I was so happy to see Mom again. I hoped she could tell me what I did wrong. "They said I was getting too big, Mom. How do I stop growing?"

"I'm a golden retriever and your father is part collie," she said. "You're going to be a big dog. You can't help it."

"I tried to be good, Mom, but they left me alone every day. I got so lonesome. I kept calling for somebody to come play with me. They called me 'bad dog' all the time."

"Humans don't have much patience with barking dogs, son. When you go to your next home, try to tell yourself stories to keep entertained." Mom nuzzled me. "You're not a bad dog at all. You're wonderful. As a matter of fact, I'm going to name you K-10, because I think you're one step above all the other canines. You're the only one of my puppies that I've ever named."

So that's how I got my real name, and no matter what people call me when they adopt me, I call myself K-10.

The girl tugs at a tangle with the brush and brings me out of my daydream. "There, look how nice and fluffy your coat is. Fluffy would be a perfect name for you. I think I'll write that on your card."

Aw, *Fluffy*? That's the worst name yet. Sounds like a cat—a *girl* cat.

She spends some extra time fussing with the top of my head. "You've had a hard life, haven't you, Fluffy? I can comb some of the longer fur over to hide that split in your ear. There, that's better. Can't hide the scar on your nose, though."

Split ear? Scarred nose? I guess those fights I was in left their marks. Next time I see my reflection in a puddle, I'll have to check myself over.

The girl gives me a trim here and there, clips my nails, then snaps on a leash and leads me out into the adoption area—a long, narrow room with cages lined up along each side. She closes the door to my cage and fastens a card to the bars. "There you go, Fluffy. You make nice for the people, and you'll be in a new home before you know it. Yes sir, you sure are a cute one."

There, she said it again. I am cute. I knew it.

There's a low woof from the next cage. "Hey, what about me?"

The girl squats down and reaches inside. "I know, Tucker. You want a home, too, don't you, boy? I'd take you home with me if they allowed pets in my apartment building."

For a second I think she understands dog talk, but then I realize she's a dog person. People like her don't catch the words, but they're good at figuring out what a dog is thinking. I've known a few dog people—like my boy, Noah.

There's a sheet of metal between each pair of cages, but ours is a little short, so I can peek around it and see Tucker. He's an old mutt—been around the block a few times. The girl pats him on the head, then leaves. She looks sad.

Tucker sees me spying on him. "Are you the guy who came in last night?"

"Yep, that's me. My name's K-10."

"What kind of a name is that?"

I explain why Mom called me that.

Tucker shook his head. "That's a mother for you. They think all their pups are perfect.

Then we end up in a place like this. They'll let the people in soon. If you look friendly, somebody might take you home."

"I've been in shelters before," I say. "I know the drill. Somebody always adopts me on the first day."

Tucker sighs. "Maybe you should be teaching me, then. I've only had one owner. His name was Jake. Then he died, and nobody in his family wanted me."

"You were with one guy your whole life? Wasn't it boring?"

Tucker looks puzzled. "It was wonderful. Jake and I were best friends."

"Listen," I say. "People will always let you down. The only one you can count on is yourself."

I can tell Tucker doesn't get this. "So why did they bring you back?" he asks.

"Who?"

"You said you always get adopted on the first day. Why did your families bring you back to the shelter and leave you?"

"They didn't leave me. I left them. The call of the open road, you know? Freedom!"

The expression on Tucker's face tells me that he still has no clue what I'm talking about, so I change the subject. "So, how long have you been here?" I ask.

Tucker droops his ears. "I'm not sure, but I think I'm near the end of my time, because that girl who just brought you in—Amy—is getting sadder every day. They don't keep you here forever, you know. If nobody adopts you, they . . ."

"Yeah, yeah, I know. Listen, you gotta spruce up your act, Tucker."

"My act?"

"Show me what you do when the people come in."

"I don't do anything."

"No wonder you're not getting any action. You gotta look cute."

Tucker's ears drooped. "Jake didn't care if I was cute. He liked me just the way I was."

"Well, that was then, this is now. You want a new owner, you have to make yourself into a new dog. Try this." I give him my best move— the full head tilt, ear perk, with big, sad eyes.

"Is that supposed to be cute?" Tucker asks.

"Forget it. I was only trying to help you.

It's no skin off my snout if nobody takes you." I go to the back of my cage, where he can't see me.

"Wait, K-10. I'm serious. I'm not sure what 'cute' is. Am I doing it right?"

I peek into his cage. "You're tilting your head too far. You look like somebody's trying to strangle you with your collar."

He straightens up a little.

"Okay, that's better. Now perk one ear up."

All of a sudden Tucker is scrunching up his face, but his ears are just hanging there. "Is it perked?"

"I can't even tell which ear you're working on."

Tucker tries again, squeezing his eyes shut and wrinkling his nose, but there is zero ear action. I'm talking not a twitch. Just then, the outside door opens and people start coming in. "Forget the ear perk, Tucker. Just look friendly. It's showtime."

He sighs. "I'll try but I don't think it'll work. I get all excited when the people start coming in, because I think maybe it was all a mistake, you know? Maybe Jake didn't really die and he'll come to get me. Sometimes I even see shoes like his, but when I look up, it's never Jake."

"Give it one more shot," I say. "Today's your day. I can feel it."

The people are coming by our cages now. There are a lot of families with kids, so I don't go into my act for them. I still have a soft spot for kids, but I've never found another Noah.

Then I see them coming in the door—a mother and two boys. One is kind of young, the ear-pulling, ride-on-your-back age, but the older one is a dog kid. I can spot one three driveways away. Sure enough, he sees me and comes running over. "Look at this dog, Mom. He's perfect."

He looks almost familiar. I can't believe it. At first I pull a Tucker, getting all excited, thinking it's Noah, but then I sniff his scent and know it isn't. Still, my heart speeds up a little.

Tucker woofs. "Looks like you got one already, K-10."

I can't take my eyes off the kid. "Yeah, maybe," I whisper. I put my front paws up on the bars of my cage, so our eyes are almost level. The mother is dragging the smaller kid farther down the line. "Not that one, Timothy. He's just a mutt."

Uh-oh. Can't let this one get away. The words *forever home* pop into my head. That's what Noah's family said they were. Well, that one didn't work out, but maybe...just maybe. I pull back my lips in a smile. This does not come naturally to me, but it's something I learned a few shelters ago from a Samoyed.

"But, Mom, he's smiling! Come see."

"You think they're going to take you?" Tucker woofs.

"I hope so," I say. "He looks just like my boy, Noah."

I'm sorry I said that out loud. Don't want to jinx it. Timothy and I are staring eye to eye, soul to soul, and I know that this kid and I could be best friends. "Tell your mom you want me," I say. "Tell her I'm your dog." I lean in and lick the fingers that are clutching the bars of my cage. He giggles. I love that sound. And he tastes like potato chips.

"Here's a poodle, Timothy," the mother calls out. "Your brother won't be allergic to poodles, because they have nonshedding hair instead of fur."

No-o-o-o! Not the poodle–allergy argument! I'm allergic to the poodles I've met because of their stuck-up personalities, but does anybody ever stop to think about that? Of course not.

"C'mon, Timothy," I say. "We'll have a blast. I'm the best Frisbee catcher in the whole entire world."

Timothy seems to be understanding me. Like I said, he's a dog kid.

Then his mother calls again. He turns and runs off without a backward glance. I can't believe it. He's giving up on me! No argument. No begging to take me home.

"What happened?" Tucker asks.

"That kid is no Noah. Besides, his mother had some nerve calling me a mutt."

"You are a mutt," Tucker says.

"Okay, maybe I am, but she said it like it

was a bad thing. We mutts are special, like snowflakes, you know? No two of us are exactly alike."

But I don't feel special at all. I feel like a soccer ball that has had all the air kicked out of it. Why did I let myself get my hopes up about that kid? It's amazing how humans can disappoint you without even adopting you.

I peek around to see how Tucker is doing. He's lying in the back corner of his cage with his head on his paws. "Hey!" I yell. "Look lively, will you? Nobody's going to take you if you don't attract attention."

A family walks by Tucker's cage without stopping.

"Come on, Tucker. You just let some good ones get past you."

"I know, but I can't pretend to be happy when I'm not."

"I'll cheer you up," I say, thinking of the last dog joke I heard. "Why did the beagle like to go to the psychiatrist?"

"I don't know. Why?"

"Because it was the only place he was allowed to lie on the couch."

Tucker chuckles and seems to brighten up for a second or two, then he lets his head droop. "Jake used to let me lie on the couch," he mumbles.

"Get a grip, will you? Jake isn't coming back, so snap out of it. You don't see me getting all mopey about Noah, do you? We gotta take what we can get. Here come some more people. Stand up and move out where they can see you."

"All right." He shuffles to the front of the cage.

"That's it. Wag your tail. Good. Lift that chin up a little. Nice. Turn and give them a side angle. Okay, now you're getting the idea. Work it. *Work* it!"

A little girl runs over and grabs the bars of Tucker's cage. "Look at this one. His name is Tucker. Isn't he sweet?"

"You hooked her," I tell him. "Now reel her in nice and slow. Add the head tilt—just a little bit."

"This is the one I want, Daddy. Can we take him home with us?"

The father comes over. "I don't want to get a dog with medical problems, Clare. This one has something wrong with his eyes."

His eyes? I look over at him. He has his face all smooshed up again and he's squinting. "Aw, Tucker. I told you to forget about the ear perk. Now look what you've done. You almost had them."

I coach Tucker for the next hour, but nobody wants him. Meanwhile, I almost hook a family for myself. The kid loves me, but the mother says, "That dog is too noisy. He's been barking every second since we came in here."

Now, that's a home I don't want to go to. I'm not barking. I'm trying to help a friend get a place to live. A dog person would know the difference, even if she didn't understand what I was saying.

I've pretty much given up on Tucker when this old guy comes over to his cage. I figure nothing is going to happen, because Tucker is back into his blue funk again. Sure enough, the guy walks by, then comes over and looks at me.

I start into my act, but not too lively. A geezer wants a calm dog, not some young pup that's gonna drag him around the block. Now the guy is looking at Tucker again. He's getting down on one knee and reaching a finger through the cage to scratch Tucker behind the ears. "You look just like my old dog, Rusty. Same eyes."

I check Tucker out. He's not even trying anymore. He's just looking up at the guy, sort of sad. Sheesh. All that good advice I gave him, and he doesn't remember a thing.

All of a sudden the geezer says, "You want to come home with me, boy?"

You could knock me over with a whisker. Who knew you could lie there like a lump and somebody would adopt you? Who knew?

Tucker is surprised, too. "He wants me," he says, peeking through to my cage. "You think I should go?"

"What are you, crazy? Of course you should go!"

The guy leaves and comes back with Amy. She's so excited, she's practically skipping. She gives Tucker a big hug. "I knew you'd find a home," she whispers in his ear. "I just wish you hadn't waited till your last day. You made a nervous wreck out of me." She snaps on a leash and hands it to the old guy.

As Amy is talking to his new owner, Tucker comes over to my cage. "Thanks for your help, K-10. Only trouble is, you spent so much time on me, you never got to find a home for yourself."

"Don't worry about me," I tell him. "I have a whole routine I can go into. I didn't even get warmed up yet."

"Yeah, but you're not getting any younger, you know? Most people want to adopt the young ones."

"What are you talking about?" I say. "I still feel like a pup."

"You may feel like a pup, but those white hairs on your muzzle are a dead giveaway. All I'm saying is, don't get too cocky and use up all your time. Get yourself out of here instead of helping somebody else, you hear? Look how close I came to . . . you know."

I wish Tucker remembered when he came to the shelter, because Amy said today was his last day. How long do they give you here?

A couple of weeks? One week . . . or less? But I don't want Tucker to see that I'm worried.

They start moving toward the door. "I'll be fine," I call out. "You have a nice life, Tucker."

He looks over his shoulder. "You too, K-10. A nice long life, if you catch my drift."

I catch his drift, all right. Here I think I'm the handsomest dog in the place—a sure thing to get adopted—and now I find out I look old and battle-scarred. When did that happen?

"Visiting hours are over for today," Amy says. "Thanks for coming, everybody." That's when I realize all the people are heading for the door.

And for the first time in my life, I'm about to spend a second night in the slammer.

Chapter

2

When Amy takes me into the adoption room
the next day, I'm ready to strut my stuff. I
don't care who's next to me. They're on their
own. I gotta get myself out of here.

Then I hear this female dog's voice. "So,
you think you're one step above all the other
dogs? Looks to me like you tripped and fell
down a few stairs."

"Huh?"

"Your name—K-10—I heard you telling
Tucker about it. If you ask me, you look more
like a K-5."

"Nobody asked you." I peek through to her
cage—the same one Tucker was in yesterday.
She's no young pup herself—a black Lab with
more than a few white hairs on her face. I

don't say anything, though. Mom taught me that I should always be polite to girl dogs.

"I'm Pearl," she says. "It was a nice thing you did for Tucker yesterday. Really stupid, but nice."

"If you think my name is dumb, what about yours? Pearls are white, not black."

She lifts her chin. "You've obviously never heard about black pearls. They're beautiful and rare, just like me." I'm trying to think of a snappy comeback when Pearl sniffs the air. "Uh-oh. Trouble's coming."

Just then, Amy brings in a big carton and empties it into the cage across from us. "Hmmm," Pearl says. "That's not good."

"What's not good?" I can't see what she's talking about. But then I hear them.

"It's mine."

"No, mine."

"I'm hungry."

"Where's Mommy?"

"Stop biting my tail."

"That's my tail."

"No, it's mine."

"I'm hungry."

"I want Mommy!"

"I'm *really* hungry!"

"That," says Pearl, "is precisely why I'm glad my first owner had me fixed. I never wanted to have a litter. It's just *yip, yip, yip,* all day long. Not to mention the fact that they want to eat constantly."

"I think they're kind of cute," I say.

"Oh, they're cute, all right. Very cute. And that spells trouble for you and me."

Just as I'm about to ask her why, Amy lets the people come in and I remember a litter of puppies in another shelter I was in. When there are puppies in a room, nobody else gets noticed at all. I go into my act, but not one person is watching me. They all sniff a trail right to the puppies.

"Those little puff balls may look cute," Pearl calls out to the people, "but they'll make wee-wee all over your rugs. And you might as well start going barefoot, because they'll chew up every shoe in your house." Nobody even turns around. "Fools," she says. "They'll learn the hard way."

"Hey, look at me," I bark. I prance around, sure that I'm looking cuter than I ever have in my whole life, but I'm performing to a bunch of rear ends.

"Save your energy," Pearl says. "The puppies get all the attention. Well . . . maybe not *all* the attention." She's looking past me toward the door. I see Amy come in with another carton, which she empties into the cage next to the puppies.

"What now?" I ask. Then I hear them.

"I'm cute."

"I'm cuter."

"I'm the cutest."

"Look at me!"

"I'm fluffy."

"I'm fluffier."

"Aw, kittens?" I whine. "Now I have to compete with kittens?"

"Not really," Pearl says. "Do you see anybody looking at you? You're no competition for those kittens at all."

There's a dog with a high-pitched bark in the cage on the other side of mine. "Pick me! Pick me! Pick me! Pick me!"

"That's really getting on my last nerve," Pearl says. "Hey, you with the squeaky voice. Can't you come up with a better line than that?"

The other dog is quiet for a minute. Then he starts in again. "Pretty, pretty please pick me! Pretty, pretty please pick me!" which is about three times as annoying as before.

"That does it," Pearl says. "I have to get out of here, and I can't wait around for somebody to adopt me."

"What other way is there?" I ask.

"I've been thinking about an escape plan," Pearl says.

"Can I go with you?"

She gives me the once-over. "Can you follow directions?"

"You mean like 'sit, stay, and heel'?"

"No, I mean like 'keep your mouth shut and run for your life.'"

"Sure, I can do that. What's the plan?"

"I told you, I'm thinking—which I could do a lot better if somebody in the cage next to you would close his big yap."

The "pretty, pretty please" dog is still going at

it nonstop. I can't see him because the metal barrier between our cages goes all the way to the front. He sounds like one of those small, yippy dogs—the kind that can fit into a lady's purse.

"Hey, you with the mouth!" Pearl yells. "What's your name?"

"I'm Peppy," comes the reply.

"You certainly are. Pipe down, Peppy."

"But I can't. I can't. I can't. Because if I'm quiet, nobody will notice me and nobody will pick me. Pretty please pick me!"

"They'll pick a pretty pair of peppy puppies before they'll pick you," I say.

Pearl gives me a nod of approval. "Hmmm. Nicely put, K-6. You might even be a K-7."

"Look, knock it off with the name," I say. "We have to work together, okay?"

She nods. "Fair enough. Now leave me alone so I can think."

It's pretty quiet after that, except for the puppies yipping when they get excited, which is about every other minute. Man, I can't remember ever being that young and clueless, but I suppose we all started out that way. I can hear Peppy whimpering softly to himself, "Oh, woe is me, woe is me. Nobody will pick me. Pretty, pretty please pick me."

I've given up trying to attract any attention, so I'm about to doze off when Pearl says, "K-10, come over here." She pushes her muzzle close to the space between our cages. "Now listen, here's the plan. At the end of the day, each volunteer takes two dogs at a time back to the kennel. When we're both out of our cages, we'll create a distraction and escape."

"That's your big plan?"

"Do you have a better idea?"

"Not really. But what if we're not together? What if one of us is still in the cage?"

Pearl sighs. "Do the math. The first ones out will be Peppy and the dog next to him. Then it's you and me."

"But how do we get outside? All the doors are locked, aren't they?"

"Not the one at the far end of the room. That's a fire exit, and it opens by pushing on the bar. It sets off an alarm, but humans have only two legs to our four. We'll be way ahead of anybody who tries to catch us."

I squint at the lighted sign over the door. "How do you know that's a fire exit? You can read?"

"No, I heard Amy taking the new volunteer around this morning, explaining everything. The volunteer is an old lady and she seems pretty nervous, so it should be easy to get away from her."

"I don't know," I say. "It sounds risky to me."

"Well, then you can go with plan B."

"What's that?"

"It's very simple. You wait around until all the puppies and kittens are adopted, hope no new ones are brought in, and then find yourself a new family." She sticks her nose between the bars and whispers, "Of course, you'll probably be dead by then."

"Okay, *okay*! I get it. We'll do it your way."

I start pacing back and forth in my cage.

Peppy is trying a new line on the visitors. "Look at me! Look at me! I'm just as cute and small as the puppies, but I'm housebroken. Puppies are so much work. Take me!"

This sounds like a pretty good argument to me, but he's not getting any takers. That high, yippy voice is annoying no matter what he's saying.

Finally, visiting hours are over. We're alone with two volunteers—the old lady and a teenage kid. The lady takes the first dog out of his cage, but she leaves Peppy behind and starts walking out.

"There goes your plan," I say. "She's only taking one dog. Now what do we do?"

Before Pearl can answer, the kid calls out, "Excuse me, Mrs. Hoffensteader, we're supposed to take two dogs at a time."

"I'm sorry, Michael," she says, "but I just don't feel secure enough to handle two dogs. It's my first day, you know." With that, she goes through the door to the kennels.

Michael takes Peppy out of his cage. For the first time I see that he's a Chihuahua. He's shaking like an aspen leaf, and his eyes are bulging out of his head—not a good look for him. Michael is opening my cage now. "It's going to be me and Peppy instead of me and you, Pearl," I say. "Maybe I can run and hide, then distract Mrs. Hoffensteader when she comes back for you."

"Never mind me," Pearl says. "Just go

ahead with the plan and escape with Peppy. I'll try tomorrow."

It was Pearl's plan, and now she's letting me go instead of her. I can't just leave her here. If Peppy and I escape today, they'll be watching everybody like a hawk tomorrow and she'll never have a chance to get out.

Michael has my cage door open now, and I'm way back in the corner, trying to figure out how to make this work.

"You lost your chance yesterday by helping Tucker," Pearl says. "Don't be a fool two days in a row. Go. Now!"

Michael reaches in and snaps a leash on my collar. Maybe if I stall long enough, Mrs. Hoffensteader will be back for Pearl. Where is that woman, anyway?

Peppy keeps jumping up on Michael, then running around in circles. "Pretty please pick me!" He never gives up.

Michael drags me out of the cage. I look around. Still no Mrs. Hoffensteader. I try to ignore Peppy, who is all over the place now. Just as I think everything is lost, Michael looks at his watch. "At this rate, we'll be here all night." He reaches down and opens Pearl's cage. He's taking three of us!

Pearl shoots out just as Michael fastens a leash on her. "Run for the exit, K-10."

I lunge away from Michael, and he loses his grip on my leash. But as I'm running, I feel something tugging at my collar. That's when I see that Peppy has tangled his leash around mine and I'm dragging him along like a dogsled.

Pearl gets to the door first. She jumps up and pushes against the bar with her front feet, but nothing happens. "The door is too heavy, K-10. Give me a paw, here."

I jump, but the door doesn't give. I try again and again. Poor Peppy is bouncing like a yo-yo.

Michael yells, "Hey! Get back here!" He's right behind us, his fingers inches from my leash. Then Pearl and I hit the bar at the same time, and the heavy door gives. We tumble through the opening, and it snaps shut behind us.

"Freedom!" I shout, just before I'm caught up short and my collar almost strangles me.

Pearl looks over her shoulder. "Where is that pesky little dog?"

"He's behind the door," I croak, "along with the rest of my leash."

The alarm is clanging now. "Run and save yourself!" I yell, but then the door bursts open and Michael stumbles out, clutching Peppy and our tangled leashes. Pearl jumps on Michael and knocks him over. He drops Peppy.

I start running, but I'm dragging the dogsled again. "Peppy, jump on my back."

"I don't think I can. It's too far up. I might fall. I might—"

"Put a muzzle on it, Peppy!" Pearl grabs him by the scruff of his neck and deposits him on my back.

Peppy's sharp little toenails dig into my neck, and his yippy voice shrieks, "Oh dear, oh dear, oh dear!" directly into my left ear.

"Hold on to my collar with your teeth, Peppy!" I shout, which is a brilliant idea—not only to keep him from falling off, but also to keep him quiet.

Then Pearl takes the lead, and with the alarm bell ringing behind us, we streak silently off into the night—off to glorious freedom!

Chapter

Pearl runs nonstop. For an old girl, she sure has a lot of energy. I call out a couple of times, but she doesn't hear me. I almost pause to take a breather, but Pearl seems to know where she's going. It was a long ride to the shelter, so I have no idea where I am.

We've been running along a country road with a lone house here and there. Then at the top of a hill, Pearl turns off into the woods. I follow her until we come to a steep slope, and there at the bottom are the lights of a town.

"Here's your new home," Pearl says. "A good hiding place up here, and everything we need down there."

Peppy jumps down from my back, but his leash is still braided into mine. "Oh, goody! I'm hungry. When do we eat?"

"Do I look like a short-order cook?" Pearl asks. "I told you, everything you need is down there. All you have to do is go get it."

"I don't understand," he says. "Where's the food?"

Pearl sighs. "You don't get out much, do you? See that big red-and-blue sign? That's Bigger Burger."

Peppy looks puzzled. "What's a Bigger Burger?"

"It's a fast-food joint," I tell him.

"I don't like to eat fast," Peppy says. "It gives me a tummy ache. Besides, I don't have my little pink doggie dish. What will they put my food into?"

"Have you ever been on the loose before, Peppy?" I ask.

"I've been out on my leash. Are being on the loose and being on the leash the same thing?"

Pearl sighs. "You have no street smarts at all, do you? You don't strike me as a runner like K-10. How did you end up in the shelter in the first place?"

Peppy is trembling, turning in little half

circles. "I don't know. When my Wendy went to work, she didn't close the door hard enough to make it click. Then the wind blew it open. I went outside, just to see what it would be like all by myself. Then I decided to take a walk. The only trouble was, a big truck went by and scared me, so I started running—running very fast. I tried to find my way home, but I didn't know where it was. Then this man caught me and put me in his truck. It had pictures of dogs and cats on it."

"So nobody dropped him at the shelter to get rid of him," Pearl mutters under her breath. "That's hard to believe." She turns back to the quivering little dog. "Peppy, if you're just lost, your owner is probably trying to find you. You should have stayed in the shelter."

"Hey, but you got your freedom instead," I say. "Good for you, Peppy. You're your own dog now."

"Don't be ridiculous," Pearl says. "Do you think Peppy is the kind of dog who can make it on his own? Without his little pink food dish?"

"Sure he can. All he needs is a little practice, right, Peppy?" I notice my stomach is grumbling. We had missed our evening meal. "How about we start by getting ourselves a little grub at Bigger Burger?"

"We have to wait until it closes," Pearl says. "Three dogs will attract too much attention if the town has a leash law."

"I have a leash," Peppy says. "My real leash is much nicer than this one."

"It's a pink leash, right?" Pearl asks.

Peppy brightens up at this. "Yes! How did you know?"

Pearl shakes her head. "Pink doggie bed, too?"

Now Peppy is jumping up and down, jerking on my collar with each leap. "Yes! Yes! Yes!" he yaps. "Have you seen them? Is my home near here?"

"Stop teasing the poor kid," I say. "Pearl is just yanking your chain, Peppy."

"I don't have a chain," he whimpers. "I have a pretty leash and a soft collar with sparklies that spell out my name. Wendy puts them on me when we go for walks. I miss Wendy."

I give him a nudge. "Hey, cheer up, buddy.

You don't need anybody to take you for walks. You're free as a bird now."

Peppy's ears perk up. "Free as a bird? I can fly?"

Pearl rolls her eyes. "You started this, K-10. He's all yours. I'm going for dinner. Bigger Burger should be closed by the time we get down the hill."

She takes off ahead of us. I wait for Peppy because I have to. We're still attached. We just barely get started down the hill when Peppy loses his footing and starts sliding. I dig in my paws and hold on as he sends a little avalanche of stones down the hill in front of us. "Easy," I say. "Take it slow." I'd tell him to take smaller steps, but I don't think it's possible to take smaller steps than his. He scrambles to his feet, and we start off again.

Next thing I know, we're on opposite sides of a small sapling, with our leashes stretched out between us. This time, I'm the one who slips. As I start tumbling down the hill, Peppy's leash pulls him right up against the tree. Then *BAM!* The sapling breaks and shoots Peppy out ahead of me. We roll end over end and land at the bottom of the hill. I stand up and shake each leg to make sure it still works. My head is whirling, but nothing seems to be broken.

Pearl is peeking around a bush at the edge of the Bigger Burger parking lot. Peppy scrambles to his feet. "Where's the food?" he yips.

Pearl turns so fast, her ear slaps me in the face. "Shush. We have to wait our turn."

I look around the bush. A rottweiler and a Doberman are rummaging through the garbage from a knocked-over can.

"I've had a run-in with those dogs before," Pearl says. "I can't let them see me."

"Who are they?" I ask.

"The Doberman is Adolf," Pearl whispers. "He's the alpha dog in town, and his sidekick is Rotter. They can be vicious. We have to hide until they're finished. Then we can eat."

"I can't wait!" Peppy cries. "I'm hungry! I have to eat right now." He makes a run for half a burger that's lying on the pavement.

That's when I realize that the fall has untangled our leashes. "Peppy, get back here!"

Peppy doesn't even break his stride—if you can call his mincing steps a stride. Adolf snatches up the burger and snarls, "Out vit you."

Rotter moves up behind Adolf. "What Adolf says goes. Scram."

"Oh, yeah?" Peppy is bouncing up and down on stiff little legs. "Who's gonna make me?"

I have to stop him before those brutes eat him alive. "Peppy, knock it off. You'll get hurt."

Adolf looks up. "Who iss dot?"

"That's my friend, K-10," Peppy says. "He could beat up both of you with one paw tied behind his back."

Pearl is shaking, with her tail between her legs. I can tell she's terrified of these dogs, but she's hanging in here to help. "Go," I whisper. "I'll handle this."

Pearl stands her ground for a second, but when Rotter peers around the bush, she takes off for the hill.

Rotter laughs when he sees me. "Are you da guy who's gonna beat us up?"

"That's him," Peppy yips.

"Ooooh, vee are scared," says Adolf. "Please don't hurt us."

"See, I told you!" Now Peppy is running in circles around the three of us. "K-10 is a superdog. He got his name because he's one step above the other dogs. Ordinary dogs are just canines—K-9s, get it?"

"Oh, vee get it, all right," says Adolf. "And now your friend K-10 iss going to get it, isn't he, Rotter?"

Rotter's top lip curls up, showing his teeth. "Yeah, he's gonna get it all right, Boss."

"Look," I say. "My mother just named me that. I'm nothing special. So I'll just get out of your way and—"

"Oh, your mama named you dot." Adolf steps on my leash, so I can't move. "Isn't dot sweet, Rotter? His mama knew her son vas a superdog."

"But I'm not a superdog. You know how mothers are about their puppies."

Rotter is about a foot taller than me. His drool is dripping on my head.

Peppy is quivering with excitement. "Beat 'em up, K-10. Show 'em who's boss."

If I could reach Peppy, I'd sit on him, but Adolf still has my leash pinned to the ground. I close my eyes, partly because I'm terrified and partly because I'm blinded by Rotter's drool.

Just then, the back door of the Bigger Burger opens up. "Get out of here, you mangy mutts!" A guy comes running out, shaking his fist at us. "I'm sick of cleaning up your mess every night. I'm calling the dog warden."

Adolf and Rotter take off for the main road. I run for the hill, climb partway up, then look back. There's no sign of Peppy. Did those bullies carry him off when I was busy saving my own skin? I feel terrible. Peppy is annoying, but he would never abandon me. I'm debating whether to go look for him alone or get Pearl to help me.

"Psst! Hey, K-10." It's Peppy, peeking out from behind a tree.

"Boy, am I glad to see you," I say. "But you

almost got us killed down there. You can't mess with tough guys like Rotter and Adolf."

Peppy's big, buggy eyes are practically glowing in the dark. "Sorry, K-10. I figured you could beat them up."

"Well, you figured wrong. If we had just waited like Pearl said, we'd have full stomachs by now."

"Don't worry," Peppy says. "Look what I have behind this tree."

I follow him. There's a huge Bigger Burger bag. Must have four or five partly eaten burgers and a whole bunch of fries in it. Never could understand why human kids take one bite of food and throw the rest away. Peppy is real pleased with himself, dancing all around his loot. "While you were talking with Adolf and Rotter, I dragged this away."

"Good move, Peppy. Maybe you're tough enough to survive on the street after all. Just don't pick any more fights for me, okay?"

"I'll try not to, but Wendy always says I have quite the little temper." I can tell he's proud of this. He picks up the bag. "We'll take this to Pearl—even though she ran out on us."

"She had to, Peppy. She had a fight with Adolf and Rotter before. They would have hurt her." I look around. "Where is she?"

"I saw her run up the hill," Peppy says.

When we get to the top of the hill, Pearl is waiting for us. Peppy drops the Bigger Burger bag at her feet. She tears it open, and we all dig in.

When we've finished all the food, Pearl turns and glares at Peppy, nose to nose. "You need to stop picking fights with dogs that are bigger than you."

"Bigger than me?" Peppy says. "Who's bigger than me?"

"Everybody!" Pearl says. "Just don't pick any more fights at all."

Peppy's ears droop. "I'll try not to, but it goes against my nature." He scurries off to find a sleeping spot for the night.

"So why are you so scared of Adolf or Rotter?" I ask. "I didn't think you were afraid of anything."

"Any sensible dog is afraid of them," Pearl says. "They're monsters."

Chapter

4

Pearl and I stretch out on the grass, on the edge of the slope leading to town. It's a warm night, and we can hear peepers singing in the dark.

"Sleeping out under the stars with friends is a lot different than being alone," I say.

"Have you been on the run by yourself a lot?" Pearl asks.

"Sure. Every time I'm between owners."

Pearl raises her head and looks surprised. "How many owners have you had?"

"Well, there was the farmer where I was born, then the people who adopted me and called me Butterscotch. They brought me back to the farm because I barked. Then when Mom had a new litter of puppies, the farmer took me to the shelter, and I was adopted by a guy who named me Spike. He wanted me to bark and scare off robbers, but I was quiet. Then some guys robbed his store, so he beat me for not barking and I ran away."

"Humans can be confusing," Pearl says. "Bark. Don't bark. How were you supposed to know? So that's when you were caught and brought to the shelter?"

"No, that was a long time ago—only my second shelter. Then I was adopted by Noah's family, and I was named Champ."

"Who is Noah?" she asks.

"Oh, just a kid who owned me for a while." I feel a pang when I say his name, but I guess in the end he let me down just as bad as anybody else. "So then I went to a family who had a young girl," I continue. "She named me Peaches. I can't remember her name. But then she got bored and forgot to feed me and brush me."

Pearl shakes her head. "She didn't deserve to have a dog."

"I know. One day her mother said she had to brush the mats out of my coat before she could go play with her friends. She was mad. She hit me on the head with the brush and told me she hated me. The next time I saw an open door, I ran away."

"Not all humans are like that," Pearl says. She looks sad.

"How many owners have you had?"

"Just one family," she says, then puts her head on her paws and closes her eyes.

"What were they like?" I ask, but she's either asleep or pretending to be so she doesn't have to answer. I guess humans have let her down, too. I'm surprised that she's only had one family, just like Tucker.

I try to sleep, too, but at first I still wake up with the slightest little noise. Then I remember I'm with my friends, so I feel safe enough to close my eyes again. Even though Pearl ran away from Rotter and Adolf, I know she's really smart and could think up a way to get us out of trouble if she had to. And Peppy might not have size on his side, but he isn't afraid of anybody. So the three of us could be a tough team to beat—tougher than I am on my own.

A hoot owl wakes me up. I'm just closing my eyes again when I hear another sound. It's low and soft at first, so it can't be very close. It's a deep, rumbly growl. It's definitely an animal—a large animal. Is it Adolf? No, bigger. I bet it's Rotter. Suddenly the growl gets louder. Whatever's making that sound is getting closer . . . much closer. I hear thrashing in the bushes and sticks breaking. It's bigger than a dog. Gotta be a bear!

I strain to see in the dark. The leaves are moving on a bush not far from where Pearl is sleeping. I'm tempted to run down the hill and save myself, but I can't do that. Mom always taught me that I should be brave and protect girl dogs. I tiptoe over to Pearl and nudge her with my nose. Her eyes shoot open and she's on her feet. "What?"

"Shhh. Listen."

Pearl cocks her ear. "Oh, that. Go over and give him a poke. He'll stop."

"No way," I say. "I'm not going to poke him."

Pearl sighs. "Do I have to do everything around here?" She's heading for the bush before I can stop her.

There's definitely something thrashing around in there now, and the growl is deeper and louder. Pearl sticks her face right into the leaves. "Peppy! Quit snoring!"

"That was Peppy? Peppy with the squeaky little voice?"

Pearl pulls her head out. "What did you think it was? A bear?"

"No," I say. "Of course I knew it was Peppy all along. I just didn't want him waking you up with all his noise."

"Uh-*huh*," Pearl says. "So you woke me up to tell me that?"

I don't have an answer. Peppy comes out from under the bush, his usually buggy eyes squinty with sleep. "Why did you wake me up? Is it time to eat?"

"No," Pearl says. "It's time to sleep."

"That's what I was doing," Peppy says. "I was having a good dream, too. I was a grizzly bear, and I was chasing Adolf and Rotter."

Pearl turns around about half a dozen times to find her sleeping spot again. "That's nice, Peppy. Now go back and dream that you're something small—a bird, maybe."

"Okay." He trots obediently back to his bush.

"And K-10?" Pearl says. "Next time some noise scares you, keep it to yourself."

I'm about to make an excuse, but she opens one eye and shoots me a look, so I keep my big yap shut. Then I settle in and fall asleep to the sound of Peppy's snores—this time a high-pitched whistle. I can tell by the look on his face that he thinks he's flying.

The next morning Pearl wakes us with breakfast, if you can call it that. "Come and get it! Fresh possum."

"Fresh? It looks like roadkill."

"Of course it's roadkill. You think I'm going to run after one of these things and bring it down myself? This is fast food."

"Apparently not fast enough to make it across the road alive," I mumble.

Peppy dances around Pearl's offering. "Are there any small pieces? I don't think I could chew anything that big."

"Peppy," Pearl says, "do you have teeth?"

"Of course I have teeth—nice sparkly ones, because Wendy brushes them every day."

"Then use them." Pearl demonstrates by

gnawing off a big hunk of possum. "Sorry I don't have a little pink bowl to put it in."

Peppy takes a dainty nibble. Not me. Never could get into roadkill. I'm a garbage man myself.

Peppy wrinkles his nose. "Wendy always fed me Doggy Delights. It came in eight different flavors and she warmed it on the stove for me. Turkey with chestnut stuffing is my favorite."

"Then you'd better hope a wild turkey runs in front of a truck," Pearl says.

"It's not the same as Doggy Delights," Peppy whimpers.

"You know what, Peppy?" Pearl says. "I think our number-one job today should be to find your Wendy. As a matter of fact, I think we should start out right now."

"Thank you, Pearl!" Peppy cries. "That's very, very nice of you."

Pearl rolls her eyes. I can tell she's doing this more for herself than for Peppy, because he's getting on her last nerve.

We head down the hill into town. As we pass Bigger Burger, I look around hopefully for some leftover food somebody has tossed aside, but it's early and people are just driving up to the window to pick up their breakfast and coffee. I sure could go for a burger and some fries right now.

As we set off through the town, Peppy's little toenails are making a *tickity-tick* sound on the sidewalk. Pearl is in the lead. "Do you think this is the town where you live, Peppy?"

"I don't know."

"What did you see on your walks with Wendy?" I ask.

"Grass, mostly. And tree roots, and the bottoms of fire hydrants. It looked the same as this."

Pearl stops in her tracks. "What about buildings? Do you recognize any of these houses?"

"I don't remember any houses. Only grass."

"For heaven's sake, didn't you ever look up?"

"Peppy's a lot shorter than us," I say. "Maybe that's all he can see."

We approach a school playground, and some of the kids come over to the fence. "Oooh, look at the cute little dog," one girl says. "Are you lost, little doggie? Can I take you home with me?"

"Here's your chance for a new home, Peppy," Pearl says.

"I don't want a new home. I want my Wendy."

Just then a woman comes over to the fence. "Stay away from those dogs, Tiffany. They're strays. I should call the dog warden."

"But they have leashes on," Tiffany says.

"Then they're runaways," the lady says. "I'm still calling the dog warden."

We take off and don't stop until we can't see the school anymore.

"What's the dog warden?" Peppy asks.

"It's the guy with the truck who took you to the shelter," I say.

"The one who took me away from Wendy? Oh no! Oh no!" Peppy starts running in circles around us.

"He's the one who can get you back to Wendy," Pearl says. "She's probably looking for you right now. K-10 and I can't go back to the shelter because nobody wants us."

"Speak for yourself," I say.

"Ex*cuse* me!" Pearl says. "I forgot about all

those people at the shelter who were fighting over you, wanting to take you home."

"You don't get it," I said. "I like being on my own. I don't want a home."

Pearl nods. "You keep telling yourself that, K-10. One day you might start believing it." She heads off down the sidewalk but is pulled up short by her leash. Then I feel a tug on my collar. When Peppy was running around us, he got our leashes all tangled together. "Now look what you've done, Peppy," Pearl says. "We can't walk around town like this."

"I'm sorry," Peppy says. "I'll fix it. I came through this way." He ducks under Pearl. "No, that's wrong. It must have been through here." He squeezes though a loop in my leash. "That's not right. Maybe I should go through . . ." He runs around a small tree, and now we're not only attached to each other, but we're tied to the tree.

"Cut it out!" Pearl yells. "You're making it worse."

All of a sudden, we hear a low woof. "K-10, is that you?"

Chapter

Tucker is peering at us through a white picket fence. "What are you guys doing here?"

"Hey, Tucker," I say. "Is this where you live now?"

"Yes, this is my new home. Why are you hiding in that bush?"

"We're not hiding," I say. "We're all tangled up in our leashes."

Peppy is burrowing under me. "Excuse me. Excuse me. I need to get through here. Coming through. Coming through." I can feel a new loop of leash tighten under my belly.

"Peppy, don't you dare move a muscle!" Pearl says.

"I'll call Bill," Tucker offers. "He's the guy who adopted me. He'll get you untangled."

"No!" Pearl says. "He might send us back to the shelter."

But Tucker doesn't hear her. He runs over to the house and starts yelping at the door. "Help! Help! Bill! My friends need help."

The door opens. "You want to come in already, Tucker? I just let you out a minute ago."

"No, my friends need help. Over there, by the bush." He runs halfway across the yard to show Bill where we are.

"Oh, you want to play, do you? Here, fetch this stick." Bill tosses a stick toward the other side of the yard.

Tucker keeps heading for us. "No, over here, Bill. Help my friends."

"Oh, so you want to go for a walk, do you? I'll go get your leash."

"I guess old Bill never saw any of those old Lassie movies," Pearl says. "He's not too swift with dog sign language, is he?"

"No, but he's nice to me," Tucker says. "Just as nice as Jake was."

Now Bill is coming out of the house with a

leash. "Here we go, Tucker. We'll take our morning stroll."

"Not now!" Tucker woofs. "Come this way!"

Bill comes through the gate and tries to get Tucker to head in the other direction. Tucker may be old, but he's strong. He starts dragging Bill toward us.

"Whoa! I mean *heel.* Is that what the girl at the shelter told me to say? Or is it *knee*? I know it's some body part, but I can't remember . . . *ankle,* maybe? I never did this newfangled obedience stuff with my old dog, Rusty." Bill is pulling on the leash, trying to get Tucker to turn around. "All right, you win. We'll go your way. Wait! What's this?" Bill has spotted us. "Aw, who did this to you poor pups? Some kids playing a prank?" He bends down to look at our leashes. "You've got quite a mess here. Let's see if I can figure it out."

"Just unhook our leashes," I say.

"Oh, he's going to get that all right," Pearl says. "He can't figure out Tucker yelling 'Help!' but 'unhook our leashes' will come through loud and clear."

Since Peppy is the smallest and easiest to handle, Bill is trying to work him over and under the loops of leash. As far as I can tell, he's making things worse. Tucker comes over and takes the hook of my leash in his mouth. He shakes it a bit so it jingles.

Bill doesn't get the hint. "Now don't you be getting in the way, Tucker. I'm trying to help these poor dogs."

Pearl puts her head on her paws. "Nice try, Tucker. You might as well lie down. I think we're all going to be here for a long time."

"Big deal," I say. "We don't have anyplace we have to go."

"Speak for yourself," Pearl says. "I have something important to do, and I've spent too much time here already. You help Peppy find his home. As soon as I get loose, I'm out of here."

"Out of here? Where are you going?"

Bill has been working at tangling us up some more, then he suddenly says, "I have an idea. I'll just unhook your leashes."

Three snaps and we're all free. Before I can say anything, Pearl takes off down the road. I wish she had told me what important thing she had to do. Maybe I could have helped her.

For the second time, I'm ready to abandon Peppy, but I just can't make myself do it until I'm sure he's safe. What if Bill takes Peppy back to the shelter and Wendy doesn't come in to find him? What if nobody wants to adopt him? What if his time runs out and . . . well, I'm just not going to let that happen.

Bill watches Pearl disappear around the corner. "Too bad your friend ran off. I was just going to get some breakfast for you."

Now, *that* gets my attention. When I'm on the loose, the one thing I always manage to get is breakfast. And I'm not talking about day-old pressed possum, either.

Peppy and I wait inside the fence with Tucker. In a couple of minutes, Bill comes out with two big dog bowls—one for food and one for water.

As soon as the food dish hits the ground, I'm slurping up my first bite.

Peppy minces up to the bowl and sniffs. "What is that stuff?"

"Some kind of kibbles," I say with my mouth full. "Tastes great."

"Excuse me," Peppy says, "but we shouldn't be eating out of the same dish. That's unsanitary."

"Are you kidding? Last night you were dying to get your snout into the Bigger Burger garbage after Adolf and Rotter had been drooling all over it. There's not going to be any pink dish, Peppy, so you'd better dig in."

Peppy sighs. "Food just tastes better in a pink dish." But he comes over and daintily picks up one kibble with his teeth. I back off to let him eat. He chews like a chipmunk, wrinkling up his nose with each bite. At that rate, I figure there will be plenty left when he's finished.

I go over to sit with Tucker by the back steps. "Where's Bill?"

"I don't know. He was mumbling something to himself, then he walked off down the road. Wait—there he is."

Bill comes through the gate holding a piece of paper. He goes over to look at Peppy, then at the paper. "I thought I recognized you. I saw this picture taped to a telephone pole yesterday. You must be Peppy. Your owner, Wendy, misses you a lot. She says, 'Heartbroken. Have lost my Peppy, the best little dog in the world. If you find him, please return him after 5:30 to Wendy at 254 Hyacinth Street.' She has her work phone number listed here. I'm going to give her a call to put her mind at ease."

"Wendy? He found my Wendy? I'm going back to my Wendy?" Peppy is bouncing around the yard like a Ping-Pong ball with ears.

I figure he's too excited to eat any more, so I polish off the kibbles, take a long drink of water, and go stretch out with Tucker under the shade of a tree. I feel better now that I know Peppy will be going back to his Wendy. The more I think about it, the madder I am at Pearl for running out on us again, though. What did she mean about having something important to do? What's more important than your friends?

I tell Tucker about how we escaped from the shelter. He tells me how much he likes living with Bill so far. "Bill might take you in, too, K-10. He loves dogs."

"Thanks, Tucker, but being owned by somebody isn't the life for me. I don't like forced marches on a leash. I want to go where I want and stop and sniff whatever I feel like. Nobody to answer to."

"Nobody to care about what happens to you?" Tucker asks.

"Sure. I'm fine on my own. Now that I won't have Peppy to watch out for, life will be easier. He's a real paw full."

"What about the other dog? The one who ran away?"

"Pearl? Oh, she's a loner, too. Can't count on her for anything. We're just alike."

Tucker shakes his big shaggy head. "You're not like that, K-10. You helped me find a new home, and you watched out for Peppy. You care about a lot of things. You're not the big, bad junkyard dog you pretend to be."

"What makes you think that? We've only spent—what—three or four hours together?"

"You can tell a lot about a dog in that length of time," Tucker says. "There's more to your story than you're letting on. You had a human you really cared about, didn't you? Is it that boy, Noah, you mentioned in the shelter?"

All of sudden he's looking at me with these wise eyes. Wise, my haunches. A few days ago Tucker was an idiot, with no idea how to find a new home for himself. And now he thinks he knows everything about me. Yeah, right, like I'm going to tell him anything.

Bill comes out the door. "Wendy's all excited about seeing you, Peppy. As a matter of fact, she's leaving work right now to come get you."

"Wendy's coming! Wendy's coming! Wendy's coming!" Peppy is pogo-sticking all over the yard. Who knew a little dog could jump that high?

It's not long before I hear a squeal of tires. A pink car zooms around the corner and slams to a stop in front of the gate.

"Peppy! Mommy's here!"

I've never seen anybody quite like Wendy. Everything she's wearing is either pink or sparkly.

Peppy does a flying leap into her arms. "Wennnndeeee!" he shrieks.

"Oh, my best little Snooky Pookums. Mommy's darling little Peppy Poo!"

Wendy is bouncing up and down and crying, and Peppy is licking her face like a melting ice cream cone. In all the confusion, Wendy has left the gate open.

This is my chance to escape. I have a fleeting thought that life might be okay here with Tucker and Bill. The second-best home I ever had was with Ralph, an old guy who took me in when I was on the run. He called me Buddy. I'd probably still be there, but he got so he couldn't walk by himself anymore. Then his family came and moved him to a place called a nursing home. Ralph told them they needed to find a home for me, but they ended up taking me to a shelter. I didn't see that one coming, or I would have run off before they could catch me.

So I'm thinking of staying here for a while, but why let Bill get to like me and then take off on him? No, it's better to make a clean break now. The only one who sees me slip though the gate is Tucker. He opens his mouth, then closes it without saying anything. As soon I take off down the road, I get that glorious feeling of freedom. My heart is about to burst with pure joy. No Peppy, no Pearl. It's just me on my own, the way I love to be.

I stop and read the pee-mail at every tree and mailbox for the next three blocks. There are a lot of messages from Adolf and Rotter, telling everybody how tough they are. One even says, "K-10. Watch out. We're coming after you." That's a bunch of baloney. If they really wanted to get me, they wouldn't be advertising it for every dog in town to read. They don't scare me. No, sir. Not one single bit. That's what I keep telling myself.

I trot on down the street and stop to read the messages at a fire hydrant. There's one for me. "K-10, if you're reading this, you're free, the way you like to be. I hope I see you again sometime. Your friend, Pearl."

Pearl gets it. This is the way dogs were meant to live—not all tied up to people like Peppy and Tucker. I'm happy at last.

The only thing I can't figure out is why— after stuffing myself with all that food at Tucker's house—I have just the tiniest empty feeling in the pit of my stomach.

Chapter 6

After I left Peppy and Tucker yesterday, I came back to our hiding place on the hill. I thought Pearl might have come up here, but she didn't. This is where I'm staying, but not because I think Pearl will show up. It's just a good spot, where I can watch what goes on down in the town.

I didn't sleep much last night. Now that nobody has my back, I need to stay alert in case somebody is trying to sneak up on me. That's okay, though. Freedom doesn't come without a price.

My stomach is rumbling. Time to find some food. When I was running loose before, I usually found some person with a soft heart to feed me. Old ladies were the easiest marks. I'd follow one home from the grocery store, then sit outside her back door and look cute and hungry until she got the hint. Only trouble is, I haven't found a likely looking old lady in this whole town.

I can see some cars in the Bigger Burger parking lot. No chance of knocking over a garbage can with all those people around. I'll just watch and wait until they close. I try to remember how I got food the other times I was on my own.

After I was Butterscotch, I wasn't on the road at all, because my people took me back to the farm. Then the farmer took me to a shelter and I was adopted to be Spike. When I ran away from there, I was loose for maybe a week. I ate mostly garbage then. That's how I was caught, going through the garbage can next to somebody's garage.

Then I was adopted and became Champ for . . . well, I don't know exactly how long. Noah was a little tail-pulling kid when I first got there, but he'd been going to school for quite a few years by the time everything fell apart. It still hurts my heart to think about that.

So after being Champ, I went to the shelter

and then I was Peaches. When I ran away from there, I was loose for a couple of weeks. I was doing the garbage-can routine again, but I was more careful that time. That's when Ralph took me in and I became Buddy. So after Ralph's family took me to a shelter, I was Harley for a couple of days until I split. And now I've been free for . . . what? Three days?

No wonder I'm not so good at finding food. For all my talk about how much I love being free, I haven't been on my own all that much. That surprises me as much as when I counted up how many shelters I've been in. I've had six names and six owners, and every single one of them let me down. No wonder I don't trust humans.

My stomach is really hurting now. I can't wait until the Bigger Burger closes. I decide to go out to the mountain road to see if there's any fresh roadkill. If I'm going to survive on my own, I'll have to learn to eat that stuff.

I sniff along the edge of the road for quite a distance until I see a squirrel up ahead, all nervous and twitchy at the edge of the road. And way beyond him, I hear a truck rumbling toward us. Good timing! I slip into the shadows where I can watch without being seen. Maybe really fresh roadkill would taste okay. I hold my breath waiting for my breakfast to be served. The squirrel starts out into the road, then changes his mind and darts back to the edge. *Come on, squirrel. Get back out there.* He can't see the truck from where he is. He's creeping out again, his fluffy tail switching back and forth. He's pretty young to be on his own. Didn't his mother teach him about the dangers of being in the road?

The truck is almost here. I close my eyes, but then I can't stand it. "Truck!" I bark. "Run!"

The squirrel hears me and streaks into the woods just as the truck roars by. I'm almost knocked over by the whoosh of air from its wheels. So much for breakfast. Oh, well, that puny squirrel wouldn't have had much meat on his bones. Besides, he was just a kid. You can't eat something like that, for Pete's sake.

The squirrel incident has made me rule out roadkill as a food group, so I go down into town and look around. The thought crosses my mind that I could go to Tucker's house for food. I'm sure he'd share with me, but that would be cheating. Either you go for the leash and collar and a full belly, or you choose independence and a twinge of hunger now and then. Can't have it both ways.

I pass the Bigger Burger and keep on going down the sidewalk—then I get a whiff of fresh bone. I follow my nose to a yard with a hedge around it. Sure enough, when I peek through, I can see a big ham bone with some good hunks of meat left on it just lying there on the grass. I look around for the dog it must belong to, but nobody's there. Still, I check again as I sneak into the yard. Whoever owns this bone is nowhere to be seen or smelled, so I'm on that thing in a flash. My plan is to grab it and hightail it out of here, but there's this big juicy hunk of ham hanging from one end, and I'm afraid it'll drop off if I don't chew it up right now.

I grab the meat in my teeth, but it's attached better than I thought. It's not coming loose, so I hunker down and turn my head to gnaw at it with my back teeth. Just then the sun fades and I hear the low rumble of thunder. A storm must be coming in. I'd better grab the bone and run for the top of the hill before it hits. Wait! Something's fishy here. There isn't a cloud in the sky.

Oh, man. It's not a storm at all. The sun is being blocked by a huge yellow dog, and the thunder is the growl coming from his throat. I drop the bone and run for my life, hoping that this monster is on the end of a chain.

He isn't. He's right behind me, but maybe he's been trained not to leave his yard.

Nope! He's charging down the street after me. I don't want to lead him back to my hiding place, so when I get to the corner, I make a tight turn away from the hill. There's gravel at the edge of the road, so I take about six scrambling steps in the same spot before I get enough traction to charge ahead. The yellow monster is clumsy turning around, which gives me a little more of a lead. I turn down an alley that runs behind some stores, but when I get to the end, there's a tall wooden fence.

I double back to give myself a running start, then head for the wall at full speed. I take off, using all the strength in my back legs to propel me up, up, and over . . . oh no! I splat into the wall about a foot from the top. I'm clawing with all four paws now, trying to dig in. But the wood is too smooth. There's nothing to grip. I slide to the bottom, my nails leaving wiggly stripes on the wood all the way down.

I look over my shoulder. Here he comes! He's not yelling anything at me—just snarling. Now I'm leaping at the wall, hoping each jump will get me closer to the top.

It's working. I'm higher, higher. This is it! I get one foot over the top, and I'm scrambling like crazy with my back feet. Okay, both feet are over the top. "So long, sucker," I yell. That's when I feel the board I'm clutching start to give. Then there's a loud crack, and I'm falling backward. I twist in midair to get my feet under me before I hit the ground.

I land right in front of Yellow Monster. Flecks of foam stick to the corners of his baggy lips, and the sun glints off his big fangs. "Look," I say. "I never would have messed with that bone if I knew it belonged to you. It was all a mistake."

He's still snarling, and a big strip of hair stands up all the way from the top of his head to his tail. Each time he takes in a breath for a new growl, his sides cave in and his ribcage expands to the size of a garbage can. Still no words. I've never seen a dog this angry.

This calls for desperate measures. I drop to the ground and roll over, exposing my belly. "Okay, I'm surrendering, see? You win."

The snarling gets louder, and he moves toward my throat. I only have one card left. No matter how mad this guy is, this play will stop him dead, because no dog can ignore it. I pee on myself.

I wait for him to step back. He doesn't. He's leaning in, dripping flecks of foam in my face. "Hey!" I yell. "End of fight. Game over!"

He's baring his teeth! I can't believe it. He's ignoring the rules of dog combat. He's going to kill me!

I make a fast move to my feet and try to run past him out of the alley, but he's on me. His big jaws clamp on the back of my neck, and he pushes my snout into the dirt. I'm a goner!

I close my eyes and hope it will be quick. I hear a loud yelp of pain. Did that come from me? I don't feel the jaws on my neck anymore.

I'm dead.

Chapter

"Are you just going to lie zere?" a voice asks. "Or vill you be getting up and going some-vere?"

"Huh?"

It's Adolf, and as usual, his sidekick, Rotter, is with him. If I'm dead, this sure isn't doggy heaven. Mom always said if I didn't behave myself, I'd go to the other place. I should have listened to her. "What happened?" I ask.

"Vee just saved your scrawny little neck," Adolf says.

"Yeah," Rotter chimes in. "Dat guy was gonna kill you."

"I'm still alive?"

"Yah. Just barely. So are you getting up or lying zere?"

"I'm, um, not going anywhere. Not unless

I'm on your turf. Am I? Because if I am, I'm out of here."

They're on either side of me now. "Every-vere you go is our turf, so it doesn't matter," Adolf says. "Vee vas just talking about you yesterday. Vee read your message vere you said how much you like being free."

"Yeah, that's me," I say. "Free as a little bunny rabbit hopping across a meadow. So I'll just be hopping along now. It's great to see you guys."

Adolf steps in front of me. "Now vot iss your hurry, little bunny rabbit? Doesn't seem as if he vants to be vit us, does it, Rotter?"

"No, boss, it sure don't."

I turn to run, but Rotter is behind me.

"Why do you tink he doesn't like us, Rotter? Vee are nice guys, no?"

"Oh, you're a couple of great guys," I say. "Why, just this morning I was telling one of my friends how great you guys are."

"Them friends of yours is long gone," Rotter says. "You ain't been hanging out with nobody that we seen, and we been watching you real close."

Adolf sticks his snout right in my face. "Yah. Vee vatch you every single second."

"I meant I was t-talking to . . . um . . . myself!" I stammer. I can't believe this. They've been watching me? Why didn't I see them? And why are they so interested in me, anyway? My brain is spinning like a hamster in an exercise wheel. How do I get out of this mess? I start backing up. "So, anyway, I'll get out of your way and . . ."

"Vere do you tink you're going, K-10?"

"Yeah," Rotter says. "Youse ain't even heard our deal yet, right, Boss?"

"Deal?" I ask. "What deal?"

"Tink of it as a partnership," Adolf says. "You scratch our ears, vee scratch yours."

"Thanks anyway, but I'm all set in the ear department."

"We ain't talking about ears," Rotter says. "Youse ain't much of a fighter, but we are."

I can't let them think I'm a coward. "Oh, well, if you mean that big yellow dog back there, I was about to go into one of my famous moves. In another thirty seconds, he would have been flying through the air."

Aldolf lowers his head to my level. "You are not grateful that vee saved you? Vee didn't interfere until the last possible second, but you vere losing the fight."

"That's for sure," agrees Rotter. "We saw youse waving the white flag."

"Maybe vee should say yellow flag?" Adolf's sly smile tells me that they saw me pee myself.

"Don't get me wrong," I say. "I am grateful to you guys for stepping in to help. So if there's any way I can pay you back, you just let me know."

"That's the deal," Rotter says. "Youse help us, and we'll help youse."

"Help me?"

"For example," Adolf says. "Vee vill make sure you have food every day."

I'm tempted, but even if I do help them, they might not keep their side of the bargain. I'm better off not getting mixed up with them.

"Thanks for the offer, guys," I say, "but I'm not a team player. I'm a loner, you know? I'm just going to fend for myself."

Adolf glares at me. "A foolish choice. You vill live to regret it."

"Yeah, if he lives at all," Rotter says. "So long, chump."

The two of them head off down the street— Adolf in the lead, as usual.

I sit back on my haunches and catch my breath. That was a narrow escape. The last thing I need is to be tied to Adolf and Rotter. Something tells me they would be worse than any owner I ever had.

I spend the rest of the day looking for food. Doesn't anybody keep garbage cans out in the open anymore? The best I can do is drink water from the creek that runs under a bridge at the edge of town. I've used water to make me feel full before. It works for a little while, but then the hunger pangs always come back worse than ever. I need to eat something to keep going. When I put my head up from drinking, I catch a scent of meat. I have to be careful this time. I'm not falling for the trick that got me taken to the shelter. I sniff for human scent, but I don't catch any. I figure whatever it is has just been run over, because there's also the smell of fresh blood. I start trotting along the road, but the scent trail makes me turn off into a field. Maybe the animal was hit by a fast-moving truck and was thrown a distance from the road.

I'm trotting through some tall grass, still sniffing the air, when I see them—three coyotes tearing at a deer carcass. The leader raises his head. He sees me and snarls. The other two spot me, too. I start backing away slowly, making sure not to look at them directly. That should let them know I'm not a threat—not going to steal their food.

Then the leader stands up and takes a couple of slow steps toward me. Uh-oh. This doesn't look good. If the other two join him, there's no way I could win a fight. My only chance is to run for the town and hope they turn back. Coyotes and people don't mix well, so they usually stay out of sight.

Uh-oh! Here come the other two coyotes now. I'm out of here. I'm partway across the field when two dark shapes run out in front of me. I can hear the first three coyotes coming behind me. I'm cornered!

"Have you ever vatched a pack of coyotes tear a dog apart?" I know that voice. What a relief! These last two shapes in front of me aren't coyotes at all. They're Adolf and Rotter.

"No, I ain't never seen dat, Boss."

"Vell, they usually slit the belly vide open."

Adolf's remark makes me shiver. "Boy, am I ever glad to see you guys," I say. "I could use a little help with these coyotes."

"This is exactly what vee vere talking about earlier today, isn't it Rotter?"

"Yeah, Boss. Dat was our deal, protecting K-10 from stuff like coyotes."

"Thanks, guys," I say. "I sure am glad you came along, because I thought I was a goner." I look over my shoulder. The three coyotes are frozen in place, waiting to see what Rotter and Adolf will do next.

"Vee vould have been glad to help you if you vere in our pack, but since you aren't, this fight iss none of our business." Adolf turns to leave, and Rotter follows him. I hear a growl from one of the coyotes behind me.

"No, wait!" I bark. "I've been thinking it over. I was wrong. I'll join up with you!"

"You turned us down," Rotter says. "Ain't nobody never said no to us, right, Boss?"

"Please!" I cry. "I made a stupid mistake. I'll do anything you want."

Adolf looks back. "Anyting?"

"Yes! Give me one more chance."

Adolf glares. I can hear the coyotes moving in closer. If Adolf and Rotter leave, I'm coyote breakfast.

I hold my breath. Then my stomach sinks as Adolf turns and starts walking away. For the second time today, I'm about to be killed, but now there's nobody to save me.

Then Adolf says, "Rotter, take care of K-10's little problem."

"Right, Boss." A hundred pounds of solid muscle barrels past me and scatters the coyotes like empty hamburger wrappers in a tornado.

I'm saved.

Chapter

After Rotter chases off the coyotes, he comes back to Adolf. "Dat was fun, Boss. You got any more animals I can chase? Because I'm a real good chaser."

"That vill be enough, Rotter," Adolf says. Then he turns to me. "Come vit us." The two of them start trotting toward town. I follow for now, but as soon as I see the right opening, I'm getting away from these two.

As if he's reading my mind, Rotter looks over his shoulder. "Youse better not be thinking about taking off."

After what I just saw with Rotter and the coyotes, I know I wouldn't stand a chance of getting away. Rotter looks big and clumsy, but he runs like the wind.

A short way into town, we pass through a

park. A mother sees us and rushes over to the sandbox to pick up her little boy. Sheesh! Does she think I would hurt a little kid? I love kids. I slow down to wag my tail at them to show that I'm friendly.

The kid smiles, but the mother yells, "Shoo! Get out of here!" The kid starts crying, so I turn and run.

Adolf and Rotter flank me in seconds. "You vill stay vit us," Adolf says. "No side trips."

"Oh, sorry!" I'm going to play along with them, mainly because they scare me half to death. But also, if Rotter and Adolf are my only hope for a good meal, I'm going to stick to them like a tick until I can get some food into my stomach. I'm so hungry I barely have the strength to put one paw in front of the other.

I slip back into my place. Even though my legs are shorter than Rotter's and Adolf's, I match their gait, moving along in their rhythm. A terrier on the sidewalk up ahead sees us and ducks around the steps of a front porch.

This is really weird. Nobody ever hid from me before. I have to admit, it feels good to be getting some respect for a change. I hold my head a little higher but make sure my tail is riding at a lower angle than Adolf's and Rotter's. I may be in the pack, but I know my place. And I know what could happen if I step out of that place.

We stop to leave some pee-mail on the big maple in the town square. Rotter lifts his leg about ten times around the huge trunk of the tree. I follow to sniff out what he says. Mostly it's stuff about how big and bad he is, but then there's one last small squirt of a note. "K-10 is running with I and Adolf now."

Is he happy to have me in the pack? I'm going to keep one eye on them all the time, in case they decide to turn on me.

This doesn't feel like running with Peppy and Pearl. We were friends who all looked out for each other. I wouldn't mind hanging around with Pearl again, but she's evaporated like fresh pee on a hot fire hydrant. I can't find any trace of her. I hope she's been smart enough to keep herself out of the shelter.

Pearl was kind of cranky, but I liked her. I wish I'd gotten to hear her life story. She never said how long she'd been on the run after her family let her down.

Adolf and Rotter are like those guys in the black leather jackets who roar into town on motorcycles. Everybody looks up when they go by. I notice that everybody who sees us has a faint scent of fear. I think I'm giving off that scent, too.

The guys take me to a spot behind Schultz's Meat Market, where Adolf has Rotter dig up their secret stash of bones. There's even a fresh package of hamburger. Adolf bites off a big hunk of meat and drops it in front of Rotter. Then he does the same for me.

"Thanks, Adolf," I say.

"Vee are pleased to have you dine vith us. It isn't every day we have a guest, is it, Rotter?"

"No, Boss. We ain't had one since dat stupid terrier who—"

"Vee von't bore K-10 with that story," Adolf interrupts. He takes a bite of his hamburger, and then Rotter dives into his. Adolf is the boss, and he hands out the food. Rotter is second in command, and then there's me. I gobble down my hamburger. When it's gone,

Adolf keeps giving me more until I'm full. This is the best meal I've ever had.

After we finish eating, we head out again with Adolf in the lead, Rotter a nose behind, and me bringing up the rear. It feels so good to have a full belly, it's all I can do to keep my tail at a respectful level instead of waving it like a flag. Maybe being in a pack can be a good thing. Rotter and Adolf promised they'd take care of me, and so far, they're doing it. I always thought all I wanted was freedom, but I'm beginning to see that the best place for a dog to be is with other dogs. Funny, I never saw it that way before.

I notice a white picket fence up ahead and realize we're coming up to Tucker's house. Sure enough, there he is in the yard. He stands up and barks. "You guys stay away from my house. I'm the boss here, and what I say goes."

Adolf jumps up and puts his paws on the top rail of the fence. "How brave vould you be vit no fence between us, old dog? I tink not so much, yah?"

Tucker struggles to stand on his hind legs

with his front paws on the fence. I can tell it hurts his old bones to do this. "I'm not afraid!" he barks. "And I'll protect my master's property from you."

Rotter comes barreling over and hits the fence with his shoulder. The force of his blow makes the fence pull partly away from the post. Tucker falls over and lands on his back, giving out a little whimper as he lands.

Adolf and Rotter go on down the street, laughing.

I rush over to the fence. "You okay, Tucker?" I whisper.

"K-10? Are you with those creeps? What on earth have you gotten yourself into now?"

"I've . . . um . . . sorta gotten myself into a pack."

Tucker struggles to his feet and peers through the slats of the fence. "You're better than those thugs, K-10."

"I know they were nasty to you just now, but they're not all bad, Tucker. You should see the big meal they just fed me—real hamburger, as much as I could eat."

Tucker shakes his head. "They're nothing

but trouble, K-10. You'll end up back in the shelter, and this time you may not get so lucky. Why don't you stay here with Bill and me? It's a nice comfortable life. You'll get all the dog food you want."

I'm almost tempted, but I just can't put my faith in another human. Bill is old. He'll probably end up like my Ralph or Tucker's Jake, and we'd both be back in a shelter anyway. "Don't worry," I say. "I know what I'm doing."

Just then, Adolf turns and calls, "Vot are you doing back zere?"

I don't want them to see me being friendly with Tucker. They might come back and really hurt him. "I'm just scaring this mangy old mutt," I bark.

Tucker gives me this disgusted look. "K-10, what would your mother say? One step above the rest, indeed." Then he turns his back on me and walks away.

I feel like a real skunk.

Chapter

It's been almost a week since I joined Adolf and Rotter's pack, and I haven't been hungry for a single minute. I'm getting used to hanging out with them. It doesn't matter that they make fun of me sometimes, because they treat me fine.

Today we're having a lazy afternoon sleeping in the woods behind Schultz's Meat Market. Well, I've been napping, but every time I wake up, Adolf and Rotter are talking low, laughing every few minutes the way friends do. They stop talking when I wake up, so I can get back to sleep again. They're much nicer than I thought they were. The first couple of days I was afraid to go to sleep because I didn't trust them. But now I know there's no safer place to be than with Adolf and Rotter, because nobody is going to mess with them.

I can see the heat waves rising from the blacktop of Schultz's parking lot, and the smell of sunbaked tar stings my nose. But it's nice and cool under the trees, so I yawn and stretch, then doze off again.

I'm dreaming about leaping across the meadow on the farm where I was born when somebody says, "K-10, the boss says it's chow time."

"Huh?" It takes me a second to realize Rotter is talking to me.

"Silly name, K-10," Adolf says. "It sounds like kit-ten, don't you tink? Maybe vee call you Kitten from now on."

"Aw, come on," I say. "Don't call me that."

Rotter towers over me. "It's just a little nickname, ain't it, Boss?"

"Yah. Friends have special names for each other. Come, Kitten, vee go eat."

I guess the nickname is okay. After all, it shows that they like me. I'm surprised to see that it's dark and the air has turned cool. Adolf and Rotter are already trotting down the road. I run to catch up. We're headed for the Bigger Burger. We've been going there late at night, after the last worker has left. That way we can eat our fill without worrying about somebody coming out and chasing us away.

I hunker down in my usual place a few feet away from the garbage cans, where I always wait until Adolf digs out our food for us, sampling it as he goes along. He knocks over the first can, and I watch the metal lid roll in a big arc across the parking lot. Then it makes smaller and faster circles until it clatters flat. It smells like a real bonanza tonight. I catch a whiff of broiled chicken sandwich with a side of onion rings.

Adolf paws through the pile of garbage, coming up with a paper wrapper that's almost full of something. "Veil, here iss a surprise. A meatball sandvich. Dot's someting new." He nibbles the meatballs, then delicately slurps up the tomato sauce. I can tell Adolf is real refined from the way he eats. One hidden meatball drops out of the paper and starts rolling away. Adolf stops it with his paw, and for a second I think he's going to send it my way. Then he changes his mind and snaps it up himself. He eats his fill, then calls to Rotter. "Come, eat all you vant."

I can hear my drops of drool splatting on the pavement. My stomach lets out a low rumble. I can't wait until it's my turn. I close my eyes so I don't have to watch Rotter eat, but that brings in the smells even stronger—beef, ham, pork, barbecue sauce, ketchup. I can see each one in my mind as I listen to Rotter pawing through the garbage. I know I'm supposed to wait until last, but it's hard when you're hungry.

Finally Adolf says, "Your turn, Kitten. Enchoy!"

I dive into the pile of wrappers, paper cups, and napkins, following my nose to the best morsels. The irresistible smell of beef leads me to a wadded-up wrapper. I pull it apart but find only a stain of beef juice and a dab of ketchup. I dig deeper and deeper through the pile, hoping for a bite of burger, a scrap of bun, or a leftover fry. Each fragrant trail leads to no more than a disappointing crumb or drop of grease. There's no food left at all. I raise my head to complain, but I'm here alone. Rotter and Adolf have taken off.

I go through the pile a second time, hoping I've overlooked something. No luck. I make a beeline back to Schultz's and find my friends in our spot in the woods.

"Did you enchoy your meal, Kitten?" Adolf asks.

"You guys didn't leave me anything," I bark. "You ate everything!"

"Surely you're mistaken," Adolf says. "Vee vouldn't be dot greedy, vould vee, Rotter?"

"We left a lot of stuff." Rotter towers over me. "Next time, you oughta be more careful, Kitten. Eating fast ain't good for you."

"There was nothing to eat!" I growl. "What was I supposed to do? Suck on the wrappers?"

Rotter's big paw pins mine to the pavement. "You ain't blaming us because you were too stupid to find the food, are you?"

"No," I mumble.

"Und surely you vouldn't be ungrateful for

the protection vee give you from . . ." Adolf looks around, sniffing the air. "From vot-ever is out zere, vaiting to pounce on you if vee kick you out of the pack."

"Yeah," Rotter says, leaning in close, "like maybe coyotes?"

"I'm grateful," I say.

Adolf is right. I have to make sure I earn my place here. I don't understand why Adolf and Rotter aren't being nice to me anymore. It must be my fault.

I'm staying awake late tonight, trying to figure what I'm doing wrong, when suddenly I see the truth. What am I, an idiot? I'm not doing anything wrong! I was lulled into thinking Adolf and Rotter were my friends, but they're not. They purposely ate all the food tonight. I have to get out of here before they do something to hurt me.

Tucker was right. I should have stayed with him. I had two chances to do that, and I blew it both times. I'm going to sneak away tonight and go to his house. Bill will take me in and protect me. Adolf and Rotter might think they're big shots, but a human can call the shelter and get them picked up. Bill would do that, especially if he saw a couple of strays being mean to Tucker. And they already damaged his fence, although Tucker would have a hard time getting that across to Bill.

I'm crawling along on my stomach now, very slowly so I don't wake up Adolf and Rotter. Just taking it an inch at a time. When I get out of their sight, I'll get up and run. If I can just get around to the other side of this tree, I should be able to . . .

"Vere are you going, Kitten?" Adolf's eyes glitter from the light over Schultz's back door.

"Me? Um, nowhere. I must have been having a bad dream. Sleepwalking, er, crawling."

Rotter is on his feet now. "Whatsa matter, Boss? He ain't trying to get away, is he?"

"No way," I say. "Why would I want to do a thing like that?" I slink back into my spot.

"Good night, Kitten," Adolf says. "Sveet dreams."

I don't dream all night. I don't even close

my eyes. I've gotten myself into a real mess, and I'm afraid I'm not going to get out of it in one piece.

The next morning, I follow Adolf and Rotter down to the creek on the outskirts of town. We each take a big drink, and I swallow twice as much as usual just to fill up my innards. Then Adolf lifts his head from the creek and sniffs. His keen eyes scan the field across the creek and fix on something. I follow his gaze and spot it. A rabbit is nibbling on clover, then hopping along to find another good patch. He has no clue that he's being watched.

"Rotter," Adolf whispers, "I tink vee dine on hasenpfeffer this morning, yah?"

Rotter's eyes lock onto the rabbit. "I see it, Boss. I'll be right back with our breakfast."

I want to bark and warn the bunny the way I did with the squirrel that was about to be run over by a truck, but if I do, Rotter will clobber me instead. The rabbit has no idea what's coming. It's nibble, nibble, hoppity-hop. *Bam!* Rotter grabs it in his steel-trap jaws, gives it one shake, and the poor bunny's neck is broken. He comes trotting back with the limp, furry thing dangling from his mouth. I feel like throwing up.

I can't watch while Aldolf and Rotter eat their fill. They leave a little pile of bloody bones for me. I don't touch it. It doesn't matter how hungry I am. I can't eat something that was hopping along minding its own business only a few minutes ago.

I grab another quick drink, then follow Adolf and Rotter as they head out to patrol the town. We stop in the town park to read the pee-mail. I'm still looking for messages from Pearl. I think I sniff one, but somebody peed another message right over it, so I'm not sure it's from her and I can't tell what it says.

We explore a new neighborhood. Well, at least it's new to me. Adolf and Rotter seem to know where they're going.

"Hey, guys, are we eating soon?" I ask. "I'm hungry."

"It vas a bad ting to skip your breakfast," Adolf says. "Now you'll have to vait until tonight. Vee can't be tipping over garbage cans in broad daylight."

This is a part of town with more apartment buildings than houses, and they all have Dumpsters instead of garbage cans, anyway. Still, I'm sniffing around to see if something dropped outside a Dumpster. That's why I miss what's up ahead.

"Vell now, vot have vee here?" says Adolf. I spot a flash of pink beyond Rotter.

"You guys get away from me before I smash you to smithereens!"

I'd know that squeaky voice anywhere.

"Hey, Boss," Rotter says, "it's a little windup toy dog dat talks."

"Vatch out, little toy dog," Adolf says. "You'd better get out of our vay before vee step on you and sqvash you like a bug."

"Do I look scared?" Peppy squeaks, doing his stiff-legged bounce toward Adolf. "You think I'm afraid of you? Huh?"

He has this little pink coat on with sparkly letters on the side of it. Oh, brother. There's an outfit that's asking for trouble.

Rotter is laughing so hard he can hardly talk. "Don't he look stupid, Boss?" he gasps.

"Oh, yeah? Think you're a big shot laughing at me, huh? How would you like a pop in the nose?"

"Vee are only allowing you to live because you're entertaining us. Besides, vee don't fight vit puny little pretend-dogs in fancy costumes."

"Pretend-dogs? Pretend?" Peppy screeches. "I'm more dog than the two of you put together. I should warn you that I had Pampered Puppy High-Energy Breakfast this morning. My muscles are fortified with vitamins and minerals. I'm a loaded weapon."

"Peppy, sweetums! Get away from those big nasty dogs!"

I know that voice, too. I ease back out of sight so Peppy doesn't see me. I've been with Adolf and Rotter long enough to know they wouldn't stoop to fight a dog the size of a pigeon, so there's no reason to get involved.

Wendy is pretty fierce herself. "You big old dogs stop scaring my baby." She catches Peppy as he circles around to her side. As she picks him up, his little legs keep running, fanning the air.

Adolf and Rotter are falling all over each

other, laughing. Wendy stamps her foot. "You terrible dogs. You're just . . . you're just . . . mean! Mean and nasty." Wendy turns and starts running down the street, with Peppy scrambling up over her shoulder. He looks as if he's going to make a flying leap onto Rotter, who is running close behind. Now I'm a little worried that Wendy and Peppy might get hurt, so I take off after them.

That's when Peppy spots me. "K-10, is that you? Wendy, put me down! It's my good friend K-10."

Rotter is running beside me. "I knew I saw that pipsqueak before. He's your friend who picked a fight with us at Bigger Burger last week."

Adolf catches up to us. "Yah, he told us dot sveet little story about how your mama named you."

"He's just somebody I met the last time I was in the slammer, guys. He's not really a friend."

"He may be small, but he's pretty brave," Rotter says. "Maybe we should have him take your place. You ain't much of a fighter."

"Peppy's all talk and no action," I yell as we run. "He'd bail out of a fight with his tail between his legs."

Peppy hears this. "I'm not afraid of anything, K-10. You know that. Why would you say such a hurtful thing?"

I stop in my tracks. The last I see of Peppy is his big sad eyes looking over Wendy's shoulder as she disappears around the corner. I feel bad for lying about him. He's probably the bravest dog I ever met.

We drop out of the chase and let them go. "You'd better succeed on your assignment today," Adolf says to me, "or I vill find someone to replace you."

I'm finally getting a chance to prove myself. "Sure, no problem. Just show me what you want me to do. Anything. Really. Anything at all. I'm your dog. Yes, sir. What's the job?"

"He'll see, won't he, Boss?" Rotter chuckles.

"Yes, as a matter of fact, vee should take our places right now," Adolf says. "The moment has nearly arrived."

"Great," I say, "I'm ready for anything. Bring it on."

But I'm not ready at all. What if I can't do what they want? I have a feeling you don't get out of Rotter and Adolf's pack alive. I've already tried to escape, and that didn't work. If I'm going to survive, I'll have to be more like them.

As we trot down the street, a dog twice my size looks at me, puts his tail between his legs, and slinks off. Other dogs fear me, just because I'm in the pack. I'm living up to the name Mom gave me. But if Mom could see me now, would she be proud of how her son turned out? I'm not so sure.

Chapter

Adolf and Rotter take me back to our spot behind Schultz's Meat Market. "So, what's the job?" I ask.

"You vill see. Be quiet and vait."

My heart is thumping against my ribs. Whatever this job is, I can't make any mistakes. I'm surrounded by a cloud of fear scent. I move downwind from Adolf and Rotter, hoping they can't smell it. Pretty soon a truck comes into the parking lot and pulls up at Schultz's back door. I can feel Adolf and Rotter tense up, so I perk my ears and pay attention to what's going on. The driver gets out and opens the back of the truck. Wow! He's pulling out a huge side of beef. Schultz comes to the door and helps him carry it in to the store.

"Now!" Adolf barks. "K-10, jump into the truck and start throwing out the meat. Rotter, you stand guard."

"Jump up there?" I ask. "Inside the truck?"

"No conversation. Simply comply vit my instructions."

"But this isn't grabbing garbage that people threw out," I say. "This is stealing good food. If the guy comes back out . . ."

"K-10 ain't going to be no help at all," Rotter says.

"Yah," Adolf says. "Vee need to get rid of him."

"No! Give me a chance. I'm your man." I jump into the truck. I've never seen so much meat in one place in my life. I shove a carton of sausages over the tailgate. They spill into the parking lot, all attached together like a long rope.

"Vee vant big stuff," Adolf says. "Big meat vit bones."

There's another side of beef, but I can't budge it. "This is heavy. Can you guys come up here and help?"

"Push harder, veakling. Do your job."

I go around behind the beef and throw all my weight against it. It's freezing in here. The floor of the truck is a combination of ice and grease, so my paws can't grip. I try another angle to get my shoulder against the meat. Then I look up and see Schultz standing behind the truck. "Darn dogs!" he yells, and slams the truck door shut.

I'm trapped! It's pitch black and freezing in here.

"What's wrong?" That must be the driver.

"Stray dogs," Schultz says. "Two of them got away, but I trapped the other one in your truck."

Adolf and Rotter ran away? They must be hiding from the men until they can rescue me.

"I can't have a dog in my truck. The meat inspector hears about this and I lose my job. I'm letting him out."

"These dogs are driving me crazy," Schultz says. "Open the door slowly. When he comes out, I'm going to hit him with this shovel."

The door opens just a crack, letting in a shaft of light. My puffs of breath are coming out in little clouds, and I'm shaking so hard, I can hear my teeth clatter against each other. I can't see Schultz or the shovel, but I know the second I peek out he's going to split my head open.

"I don't have time to wait around," the driver says. "That dog could have eaten half of my cargo by now."

Eat? He thinks I could eat at a time like this?

The door opens all the way, and there's no time to think. I make a dive. I see the shovel coming down. There's a sharp stinging pain on my shoulder, but it's not enough to stop me from running. I streak out of the parking lot and into the main street. I don't see Adolf and Rotter.

What I do see is a pickup truck. Mom always told me, look both ways before you cross a road. How could I forget that? Everything goes into slow motion. The truck's shiny bumper is getting closer. I can see the reflection of buildings in it—then the reflection of a dog's face.

It's my face.

Chapter

Brakes screech. Some guy yells, "Watch out!" There's a thud. I tumble end over end, stopping when I slam against the trunk of a tree. I gather my legs under me and try to stand up. I'm wobbly, but everything works. I'm okay.

The guy driving the truck gets out and is heading for me. Gotta get out of here. I'm running. Don't know why. Don't know where. I'm running. A dog is yipping in pain. *Ki-yi-yi-yi.* Somebody's hurt bad.

Something warm is dripping in my eyes. Hard to see. Smells like blood. Gotta keep running. More yelling behind me.

I'm scrambling up a hill. Got to get to the top. I set off a shower of stones and start sliding. Can't fall. Gotta keep climbing. Can't stop. I get a foothold.

Ki-yi-yi-yi. There's that cry again. Right behind me. No—not behind. It's coming from me! More climbing. More slipping.

Finally at the top. I lie down and look over my shoulder. Nobody followed. Now that I've stopped, everything hurts. I'm bleeding. The scent of blood could attract a wild animal. Not safe here. I should check myself out—move on—but I'm sleepy. Can't stay awake. Just need a short nap. Then I'll feel better.

I'm dreaming of the farm. Mom is here. She's licking my wounds, telling me what a good puppy I am. Telling me not to worry. "You'll be fine," she says. I wish I'd stayed on the farm when I was a pup. Gotta go look for that farm when I wake up. Gotta find Mom.

There, I'm dreaming about her again. She's nuzzling me awake. "Hi, Mom," I say. I open my eyes. It's not the farm. I'm at the top of the hill, but I'm not alone. Is it a wild animal? I try to get up, but I'm too weak.

The animal pushes me back down. "Lie still," it says.

I think I know that voice. Could it be? "Mom?"

"Call me that one more time, and I'll leave you here for the coyotes."

My eyes are blurry. All I can see is a black shape. Then I catch the scent. "Pearl? Is it you?"

"It's me, K-10."

"I thought you were gone."

"I went off exploring," she says. "I found what I was looking for, so I came back for you. You managed to get yourself in a heap of trouble while I was gone."

"I joined Rotter and Adolf's pack," I say.

Pearl is licking a wound on my shoulder. "Why would you do a stupid thing like that?"

"They promised to protect me and make sure I have enough food."

Pearl sits back on her haunches. "Oh, really? So how's that working out for you?"

"Okay, I guess."

Pearl snorts. "They're doing a fine job of protecting you, except from the guy who clobbered you with the shovel and the truck that ran you over. Adolf and Rotter were right by your side fending off danger, I assume."

"I can't remember. I know they tried to help."

"They didn't try, K-10. They deserted you. I saw the whole thing."

"Rotter and Adolf ran off?"

"Like a couple of greyhounds sprinting for the finish line."

"But I'm sure they're worried about me."

"Worried sick," Pearl says, checking me over for more wounds. "That's why they're out in the woods behind Schultz's right now, pigging out on sausages."

"They'd be taking care of me, but I ran off. They don't know where I am."

"Correction," Pearl says. "They don't *care* where you are."

"You don't understand, Pearl. I'm part of their pack."

Pearl gives me this disgusted look. "Right. You're the part of the pack that's disposable. They use you to do the most dangerous job of their dirty work. Then if you get hurt—or worse—you can always be replaced, the same way you took the spot of that poor terrier who used to run with them."

"Rotter said something about a terrier. What happened to him?"

"They killed him, K-10. And laughed about it afterward. I saw the whole thing."

The thought makes me shiver.

Pearl nudges my shoulder. "Now try to stand up and let's see if anything's broken."

I struggle to my feet. Everything hurts now.

"Can you walk?" Pearl asks.

I take a few steps. "Yeah, I guess so."

"Good. I want to take you to a safer place. No sense hanging around where Rotter and Adolf can track you down again."

"Can we eat first?" I ask. "I'm starving."

"All I can find around here is roadkill," Pearl says.

"You mean possum?"

"I mean whatever is dumb enough to run out in front of a car. Yes, most likely possum. But there's real food where we're going, if you can hold out."

The thought hits me that I was dumb

enough to run in front of a truck and probably just inches from becoming roadkill myself. My stomach lurches. "I guess I can make it if it's not too far. Is it a place like Bigger Burger?"

"No. It's a campground. The people there are nice. I'm sure it's the place where I got separated from my family."

I take a few painful jogging steps to catch up with her. "Why did your family leave you at a campground? Did you do something bad?"

Pearl slows her pace. "They didn't leave me on purpose. It was a silly accident. I was inside the camper while they were packing things up to go home. Then I spotted a squirrel. I jumped out and ran after it. I didn't mean to go far—just one last dash though the woods. But squirrels can be so tantalizing, you know? They zip up a tree, spring from branch to branch." She looked up from tree to tree with a sparkle in her eye. I could almost see her imaginary squirrel zinging around up there.

"Yeah, I know. Hard to resist going after them, that's for sure."

Pearl snaps out of her squirrel trance and speeds up. "Come on. We need to keep moving if we're going to get there by dark."

"Did your family think you were in the camper when they left?"

"Of course. They were rushing around getting the three kids packed up. They probably drove for miles before they noticed I was gone."

"Kids? You were in a family with kids? Boy, I'm sure having a hard time picturing that. You don't like kids."

"It's puppies that I don't like. Kids are fine. Especially boys. We used to do cool stuff together. And their parents were good to me, too. Whenever we were in the car, they'd stop for ice cream. They always got me my own cone."

"So why didn't they come back to find you?"

"I tried to follow them, but . . . Never mind. I don't want to talk about it."

I have a million questions, but I keep my mouth shut and we walk along in silence. My mind is going a mile a minute, though. Pearl with a family of kids. Who knew?

We have to stop a few times so I can lie down to rest. At one point, Pearl spots a half-eaten bag of fries that somebody must have thrown out of a car. She gives the whole thing to me. "You don't want any?" I say. "You're not hungry?"

"Not as hungry as you are. You're the one with the ribs sticking out."

I eat every single one, then tear open the bag and lick the grease on the inside. It doesn't fill me up, but it helps me feel a little better. I have a hard time getting to my feet again.

Pearl sees me wince. "It's not much farther, K-10. You'll make it. We'll walk slowly from here." A little way down the road, she sniffs the air. "We're close. We'll take a short-cut." She heads into the woods. I follow, limping. Pretty soon we come upon a place with cars and tents. Pearl leads me over to an old shack away from everything else. "You can hide in here. It's just where they store things. Nobody will see you."

"Wait a minute. If people are friendly here, why do we have to hide?"

"I didn't say we had to hide. I said you have

to hide. One dog going around begging food from the campsites is cute. Two dogs is a wild pack, and they'll chase us away."

"Why don't I do the begging?" I say. "Looking cute is my specialty."

Pearl nudges me over to a pile of cloth bags. "You didn't even look cute before you tangled with that truck. Now you're a disaster. Lie down and rest while I'm gone."

It takes about six circles before I can lie down. The bags make a soft bed, but I can't get my sore bones comfortable. I get up and try a couple more times, then give up.

Pearl is making a big mistake, thinking that she's cuter than me. Cute is the one word that doesn't come to mind when I think about Pearl. Snarky—oh, yeah. Sarcastic—big-time. But cute is Peppy, not Pearl.

I know she's going to mess this up, so I decide to go out on my own and gather up some grub. I sneak though the shadows toward the tents. It's getting dark now. Every step hurts. I stumble and fall. Pearl had licked the blood off my head, but the bleeding has started again, running into my eye.

I see Pearl at a campsite up ahead. There are some kids gathered around her, and her tail is wagging in circles like a windmill. Never saw her tail wag before. Her face is lit from the flames in the campfire. And now she's—I really don't believe this. She's doing the whole head-tilt, cocked-ear thing. She's stealing my moves! Must have watched me go through my act at the shelter.

One of the kids is tugging on his mother's sleeve. "Can we keep him, Mom? Please?"

Now, there's a kid who could use a little biology lesson, but Pearl doesn't miss a beat. She's really working it. She's almost—well—cute! I bet these people are going to take her home, and I'll be stuck here by myself. Pearl has forgotten all about me. Okay, that doesn't matter. I'd do the same thing in her place. I'll just find another family to get food from. Not going home with anybody, though. Not joining another pack of dogs, either. It's just me, myself, and I from now on.

I hear the kid's mother say, "This dog must belong to somebody here at the campground. We'll ask around tomorrow."

"Can we name him Buster, Mom?"

Buster! Ha! Serves Pearl right for deserting a friend when he's down and out.

I see another campfire up ahead. People are sitting around talking. I practice smiling as I head for them. Supper, here I come.

I may be a little bit beat up right now, but I know I still have the old magic. Besides, this must be an easy crowd. If Pearl can use my moves and win people over, then I should have them eating out of my paw in no time. Better yet, I'll be eating out of their hands. Just the thought of food makes me drool.

A family is sitting around the campfire toasting marshmallows. The smell of them makes me drool even more.

I shake my head to fluff up my fur. There, that should cover up any scrapes on my ears. I whipped a few strings of drool onto my coat when I did the head shake, but who's going to see that in the dark with just a fire for light?

Okay, I'm getting close now, so I start prancing a little. Ouch! Man, why does everything hurt? Still, I gotta look like a young, lively dog. Kids want dogs to have energy.

Hey, one of them just spotted me. I tilt my head and smile.

"Dad! What is that thing over there?" The kid is pointing.

What thing? Where? Is something sneaking up behind me? I turn my head. Nope.

"There's nothing there," I bark. "Don't be scared. It's only shadows." I prance in place a little to show them I'm not afraid. Perk my ears up. Lookin' mighty cute here.

The father is getting up. Probably coming over to pet me, then invite me to lie next to the warm campfire. Maybe have a bite to eat. Yes sir, I still have the old charm. I give them my biggest and brightest smile.

The smaller kid starts crying. "Is it a wolf, Daddy? Is he going to eat us?"

A wolf? I turn around again and squint into the darkness, just to make sure I didn't miss something. I take a big whiff of air, but I'm not getting wolf scent. I'm getting . . . steak. Oh, yeah. Nothing like steak cooked over an open fire. Or raw, for that matter. I'm having a major drool eruption here. The steak isn't at this campfire, though. Maybe I'd better skip the marshmallows and go find the beef. I put my nose in the air to sniff where it's coming from. Okay, I have a scent trail leading directly from my nose to that steak. I do a little happy dance.

The lady is getting up now. She's probably coming over to feed me some marshmallows. I feel bad about turning down her treat. Don't want to hurt her feelings, but come on—steak? A dog's gotta do what a dog's gotta do. I smile at her, just to be nice.

"Harold, get back. That dog is baring his fangs and foaming at the mouth. And did you see him run around in little circles? He's rabid, I tell you. Stay away from him."

Running in circles? Does she mean my happy dance? And that stuff coming out of my mouth is drool, not foam, for Pete's sake. And I'm not baring my fangs; I'm smiling. Can't she tell the diff . . . *Thwack.* A big piece of firewood comes zinging through the dark and hits me in the haunches.

"Get the kids in the camper, Verleen. The dog's all bloody. Must have tangled with some wild rabid animal. Probably more of these wild dogs out here. Maybe a whole pack of them. I'm going to tell the campground owner. They should keep mangy dogs like this away from here."

Okay, people. You can keep your puny little marshmallows. I'm out of here! I know when I'm . . . *Thud* . . . ouch! . . . not wanted. Yes, sir. Nobody has to hit old K-10 over the head with a . . . *Conk* . . . hey! Knock it off!

I'm running now. Past the campfire with the steak, because those people have heard the ruckus and Marshmallow Man is yelling, "Mad dog! Mad dog!" for everybody to hear.

I'm mad all right, but not the way he means it. That idiot just cost me a good steak dinner. Well, at least a good steak bone. I'm way ahead of the people chasing me. I dive into the shack where Pearl left me. She comes in a couple of minutes later.

"What were you thinking, K-10? I told you to stay out of sight." She drops a half-eaten hot dog roll at my feet.

"I just wanted to help. I don't want to brag, but I'm really good with people."

Her eyes widen. "Are you kidding? You scare

people. You're still all bloody. Now every-body's talking about the rabid wild dog that's stalking the campground. Somebody even yelled at me when I was on the way back here. You've gone and ruined everything for both of us."

Pearl is really angry with me. Now I've done it. I'll be on my own again, but I'm not so sure I can make it without her. "I'm sorry. I just thought . . ."

Pearl whirls around to face me. "Thinking is not one of your strong points, K-10, so don't even try it. I'll do the thinking for both of us."

"You mean you're not going off and leaving me?"

She looks me straight in the eyes. "If I were hurt, would you leave me?"

"Well, no, but I thought . . ."

Her face softens a little. "We're friends, K-10. I'm not going to leave you when you need help, even though you're a major pain in the tail. Now eat that hot dog roll and get busy cleaning yourself up."

This is a side of Pearl I haven't seen before. It's not that she's turned all mushy or anything, but I know she won't abandon me. And I for the first time, I realize I wouldn't desert her, either.

The next day Pearl goes back to the family who has been feeding her. I follow her just to make sure she's all right, but I stay out of sight. The kids run over to greet her. Uh-oh. Here comes the father. Is he going to run her off? No—he's petting her. There goes her windmill tail again. Now that I know she's okay, I head back for the shed. She comes later with a piece of toast for me.

"Everything okay out there?" I ask, gobbling my breakfast in one bite.

She lies down beside me. "Yes, but while I was there, the man from the next campsite came over to tell my people about the wild dog he spotted last night. He didn't get a good look at you in the dark—said you were huge and muscular. Can you imagine?" She chuckles to herself. "Huge and muscular. Ha!" Then she gets serious. "K-10, my people say they're asking around to see if anybody at the campground owns me. If nobody does, they want to take me home with them tomorrow."

I feel a little pang of loneliness starting already. "You think they'd treat you okay?"

Pearl looks off into the distance. "I don't know. They're nice enough, but I can't help thinking about my real family. The boys must be heartbroken to lose me."

"Um, Pearl, I don't want to burst your bubble here, but if your family misses you, wouldn't they have come looking for you?"

Pearl puts her head between her paws. "I know they love me."

"But they're only humans," I say. "They don't have the same standards as dogs. If they lose a dog, they just get another one. You know, the way they get a new car every few years even though the old one still runs? They've probably replaced you with a puppy already."

Pearl shudders. "A puppy? That's like replacing the reliable family car with a crummy little plastic wagon."

"Well, it happens all the time. That's why I've never put my faith in people. They give us a food dish, a bed, and a walk around the block and expect us to give them our love and loyalty for as long as we live. It's a great setup for humans, but a rotten deal for us dogs."

Pearl closes her eyes. I can tell she doesn't want to talk anymore.

"Look, Pearl, not that I'm ungrateful for the food that you brought me, but my stomach is still rumbling. I'm going to look for garbage cans near the front entrance. I'll go way around the outside of the campground so nobody sees me. You want me to bring something back for you?"

She doesn't even open her eyes. "No, I've lost my appetite."

I feel bad that I've upset her, but it's better that she knows the score. I know she should go home with the family who wants to adopt her, but I secretly hope she'll want to stay with me instead. I cut through the woods and out to the main road. My shoulder doesn't hurt as much as it did yesterday. I worked pretty hard on cleaning myself up, so I can't smell blood on my fur anymore. I stop to check out my reflection in a puddle. I don't look great, but I'm not bad enough to scare little kids.

When I hear a truck coming down the road, I run off into the trees. I'm never getting in the way of one of those things again. Pretty soon I see the entrance to the campground ahead. The garbage cans have been left near the road to be picked up. I check to see if anybody's watching, then start through the gate. That's when I notice this piece of paper nailed to a pole. That's funny. There's a picture of a dog on it. I look closer. That's not a dog. It's Pearl! Why would they have Pearl's picture out here? I'd better tell her about it.

I get on my hind legs and take the paper gently in my teeth. It tears a little as I pull it off the nail, but you can still see her picture and all the words.

I run all the way back to the shed. Pearl hasn't moved, but her head jerks up when I come in. "What's that?"

"It's a piece of paper with your picture on it."

She sniffs it from top to bottom. "My family had this, K-10. They were here looking for me."

"Don't get all excited, Pearl. They're long gone now."

"The words may tell how to find them."

"But you can't read." My mouth opens, letting the paper flutter to the floor.

"Of course not," Pearl says. "But the people who were looking for my owners can." She picks up the paper by one corner and is out of the shack before I can say anything. I follow her, not bothering to hide this time.

Pearl runs right into the campsite, the paper flapping in her mouth.

"Hi, Buster," the kid says. "What's this?" He takes it from her. "This dog looks just like you, but it can't be, because this dog is a girl." He looks over at Pearl, then does a double take. "This *is* you, isn't it? You're a girl?"

"What does it say?" Pearl barks. "Read it. What does it say?"

Pearl's barking has brought the mother out of the tent. "What's all this racket out here? Buster, what's wrong? You're usually so quiet. You're not going to be noisy when we take you home with us, are you?"

"I can't go with you," Pearl barks. "This is from my family. Read it." She's running in circles around them.

"Buster is a girl, Mom. And she belongs to somebody. Look."

The mother reads, "Please help us find our beloved Pearl. The kids are heartbroken without her."

Pearl looks at me. "See?" she hisses. "Replaced by a puppy indeed!"

The mother pulls a tiny telephone out of her pocket and starts poking at the buttons. "There's a number here. I'm calling them. Hello, Mrs. Rinaldi? I think we found your dog."

"That's them!" Pearl barks. "That's their name. And the kids are Tony and Joey and Sam."

"Yes, that's her barking," the mother says. "She's right in front of me. We're here at the campground."

The littlest kid is hugging Pearl around the neck. "Please, can we keep her, Mom?"

The mother doesn't hear him. "Yes, I'm sure it's her. Little white spot under her chin? Wait, I'll check."

Pearl lifts her chin. "White spot right here. See?"

"Yes, there's a white spot. Okay, we'll keep her tied up until you get here. She's pretty excited, almost as if she knows what we're talking about. She even brought us your poster. Isn't that something? There's another dog here that seems to belong with her. Oh, not yours, huh? All right, then. We'll see you in about half an hour."

"They're coming!" Pearl barks. "My family is coming to get me. They didn't forget."

"Yeah, terrific," I say.

Pearl calms down and looks at me. "Oh, K-10, I'm not going to leave you alone. Maybe this family who was going to adopt me will take you instead. Do your cute act."

I walk over to the kids and give them a soft "woof." Then I give them the big-sad-eyes routine, followed by the head tilt–ear perk, but my heart isn't in it.

"Come on, K-10," Pearl whispers. "These kids really want a dog. Show a little enthusiasm. You need a family."

That's when I blurt out something that never even occurred to me before. "All I need is you, Pearl. You're all the family I want."

Pearl looks sad. "It won't work, K-10. I want to live with my family, not be on the road. And you can't stay on the run, either. That's no kind of life."

I was beginning to panic about losing her. "I could follow your family's car home and hang out near where you live. That way you could have your family and I could have my freedom."

Pearl shook her head. "You're getting older, and winter will be here before you know it. You should be inside where it's warm. And a family is a good thing." She gives me a nudge. "Go make nice with those kids. Win them over."

My heart isn't in it, but I'll give it a try, just for her. I'm moseying over to the kids when Marshmallow Man bursts into the campsite. "That's him! That's the rabid dog I was talking about! Get away from those kids, you mangy mutt! I'm getting the camp manager right now."

The mother grabs the two kids and pushes them into the tent.

Pearl gives me a shove. "Run to our hiding place, K-10."

I take off, and she's right behind me. I hear a couple of people shout at me as we streak past their campsites. One guy tries to follow us, but we leave him in the dust. We slide into the shack before anybody can follow us.

"You have to go back," I say. "What if your family comes and you've run off?"

Pearl is out of breath. She flops down on the ground, panting. "I have an idea. My family loves dogs. I bet they'll take you, too. They used to have two of us before old Smackers died."

My heart leaps at the thought of going home with Pearl and living with her family. But then I come to my senses. "Pearl, I can't live with humans anymore. I've tried it over and over, and every time they let me down. I can't trust them."

"But what about that boy you mentioned? What was his name? Noah? He loved you, didn't he? Weren't you with him a long time?"

"Yes, from the time he was little until he had been in school for four or five years. But then he left me, too. Humans are all the same."

"Why did he leave?" Pearl asks.

I want to tell her to mind her own business, but she's not going to let this go until she has an answer. "I don't know why he left. We did everything together right until the end. Then he got tired of me, just like the others."

Pearl moves in closer. "That doesn't sound right to me. Think back. Something must have happened."

"All I know is that the family was going to move somewhere else and they didn't want to take me along."

"Maybe they couldn't take you. Lots of apartments don't allow pets."

"Then Noah shouldn't have gone with them. If he was really my best buddy like he always said, he should have stayed with me."

Pearl shakes her head. "Humans aren't like dogs, K-10. They stay with their families until they're full grown. You've never seen a kid living alone in his own house, have you? Noah had to leave. He had no choice."

I hadn't really thought about that before. "Noah did have a sad scent about him that day," I say. "I remember they had all their stuff packed in a big truck, and their car was loaded up, too. Noah sat with me on the porch steps and hugged me. He didn't say anything, but I think he might have been crying."

"See? He didn't want to go without you. But who was supposed to take care of you? They weren't going to leave you on the street, were they?"

"I was going to live with the next-door neighbors, but I didn't want to. I wanted to go with Noah."

All of a sudden I could see it so clearly in my head—stuff I hadn't remembered before. "Noah's father had to practically drag him into the car. He said they had to move because of his job, and it couldn't be helped. My new owner was holding my leash, but when the car started down the road, I could see Noah pressing his hands against the back window. He was calling my name, so I tugged at the leash and ran after them, but they were going too fast for me to keep up. When the car was out of sight, I followed the scent of their tires until there was no scent left. Then I was lost."

"Noah didn't let you down," Pearl says quietly, "He had no choice but to leave."

I'm feeling better about Noah, but I'm thinking about my track record, about how one owner after another gave me up. What if I do that to Pearl's family? What if I get her kicked out, too?

"K-10, you should come live with my family now," she says.

No matter what happens to me, I want Pearl to be happy with the people who love her. "I can't go with you, Pearl."

"But, K-10 . . ."

"Don't argue with me about it. I'm not going."

She doesn't say anything more. We stay quiet for a long time in the shed. I'm looking hard at her face, so I'll always remember what she looks like. I think she's doing the same thing with me. Then in the distance we hear a car crunch to a stop on the gravel driveway. The slamming of car doors echoes through the woods. Somebody calls out, "Pearl!" She cocks an ear but doesn't move.

"Go," I say. "Don't lose your family for a second time."

She slowly gets up and goes to the door, then turns back. "I can't leave you alone like this, K-10."

I put on my happy act. "Sure you can. You know me. A few weeks cooped up in a house, and I'd be going nuts. Go."

"You sure?"

Just for a second, I'm thinking it might be worth a try. Could it be the way it was with Noah? Three boys' voices are getting closer now. "Pearl! Pearl, where are you?"

"Go to them. I'll be fine." I almost choke on the words.

Pearl gives me one last look. "I'm here!" she barks, and she's off, running like a puppy to greet them. I follow at a safe distance. The three Rinaldi boys tackle her, and they all tumble in the grass. The kids are laughing and crying at the same time. The father and mother hug her.

I'm so happy for Pearl, my heart is bursting, even while it's breaking because I'm losing my best friend.

As Mr. Rinaldi starts to put Pearl in the

car, she barks, "Wait! I have a friend. Can we take him?"

I hold my breath to see what will happen, but of course nobody understands. The oldest boy glances at me for a second while the parents thank the other family for calling them. The kid has a puzzled look on his face, and I think maybe he's going to get it. Then the father loads Pearl into the car and the kid turns and piles in with the rest of them. Within seconds, they pull away. I can see Pearl's face in the back window. She's barking, but I can't hear what she's saying. It's just like when Noah's family took him away from me.

All of a sudden I freak out. I can't let Pearl go. "No-o-o-o-o-o!" I howl. "Come back!" But nobody hears or understands me.

I have to follow them. I take a good whiff of their tire tracks so I can follow the scent if they get too far ahead of me. It's a good thing, because the car is already out of sight by the time I get to the main gate. The tracks are fresh, so it's easy to know which way they turned—the opposite direction from town.

I'm making good progress with the tracks. The scent is strong and pretty easy to follow. I keep my nose to the road, following the tires on the right side of the car so I'm closer to the edge of the road. Then a truck driver blasts on his horn, nearly scaring me out of my wits. I run for cover, only creeping back out when I can't see or even hear any more cars.

The traffic is picking up in both directions now. I must be getting close to a town. More people are blowing horns, so I have to keep getting off the road to avoid being hit. Each time several cars pass me, it's a little harder to find the scent of the Rinaldis' car. I can't lose them. I can't bear the thought of never seeing Pearl again.

I've been wasting too much time running off the road. Now I'm staying on the scent even when cars honk at me. They swerve around me at the last second—at least so far. The Rinaldis' scent mingles with too many other cars, getting fainter, but I concentrate harder and catch enough whiffs of it to tell me I'm on the right track. I can even tell where they turned off onto another road.

I see dark clouds ahead, which could be bad, because rain washes away a scent trail. But dark clouds don't necessarily mean the storm is coming this way.

Ping, ping, ping-ity splat! Big drops of rain are splashing on the asphalt now. If I keep going down this road, maybe I'll come to a place where it hasn't rained yet, and I'll pick up Pearl's trail again. At least there's no thunder and lightning.

Hey! Why is the hair on the back of my neck standing up? *Crackle, sizzle, pop, pop, pow!* Yikes! That's close. Lightning streaks all the way to the ground up ahead. I run to the nearest house and dive under the porch.

Okay, it's dark in here, but I'm safe from the lightning. I'll just curl up and . . . Wait, what's that scent? I'm not alone. "Oops! Sorry! Didn't know anybody was in here. Ouch! Hey! I said I was sorry." The thing is moving toward me again. "Back off, will you? You don't have to get all bent out of shape. I'll leave right now. Ouch. *Ouch!* AWOOOOOOOOOOO!"

Chapter

I'm running down the road in the rain again. Who would expect to find a porcupine under a porch? The quills sting my muzzle. I've heard about dogs tangling with porcupines, but it never happened to me before.

The rain is pelting me so hard, I can barely see where I'm going. The thunder and lightning scare me. I'm tempted to duck under another porch, but who knows what might be lurking there?

I just keep moving. Cars splash cold, muddy water on me as they speed by. It doesn't matter. Once you're soaked, you can't get any wetter. And once a porcupine has given you a snout full of quills? Well, you can't get any more miserable than that.

The rain is ending as suddenly as it

started. I stop to check my reflection in a puddle. I look as if I have a bushy, prickly beard. It hurts enough to make my eyes water. I try to scrape the quills off my chin by rubbing against a tree, but that makes the pain even worse.

A hound chained up in a front yard barks at me. "Hey, buddy! What happened to you? Have a run-in with a porky?"

"Lucky guess," I say.

"Happened to me once," the hound says. "Hurts something awful, don't it?"

I stop in my tracks. "How did you get the quills out?"

"There's only one way. Your owner has to pull them out one by one with pliers. Pure torture, but it's gotta be done." I'm just about to ask the hound where his owner is when he says, "Yeah, my owner was real mad at me for messing with a porky. Well, not quite as mad as when I tangled with a skunk, but that's a whole 'nother story. Anyway, he yelled at me the whole time he was yanking out the quills, then gave me a beating when he was finished."

All of a sudden, I see a mean-looking guy coming out of the house behind the hound. I take off, running.

Sheesh! Could things get any worse? I'm cold, tired, wet, hungry, and lost, with a face full of sharp quills that can only be taken out by a human owner, which is exactly what I don't have. I wish I could find the farm where my mom lives. She'd know what to do to make me feel better.

I see an ice cream stand up ahead. Didn't Pearl say her family liked ice cream? Could they have stopped there? I sniff around for their scent, but the rain has washed everything away. Wait—I'm getting something. Over here, by this little pine tree. I zero in on a pee-mail message on the ground by the trunk, where it's sheltered from the rain. It's from Pearl!

K-10, I saw you running after the car, so I hope you're still on our trail and reading this. We stopped for ice cream. I tried to run away to find you, but Mr. Rinaldi caught the end of my leash and brought me back. I have to get in the car now. I think our house is on this road. I'm not sure how far, but if you . . .

Rats! She ran out of pee. She's gotta learn how to pace herself if she wants to leave long, important messages. Okay, at least I know I'm on the right track. As I start out again, my spirits are high, except for the fact that my snout hurts so bad, I want to bite my own face off.

I keep running on the edge of the road, hoping for a scent, but there's nothing. I keep my ears tuned for Pearl's bark. Still nothing.

Way up ahead I see a dog coming toward me. Well, I think it's a dog, but the way my luck has been running, it's probably a wolf. When the animal gets closer, I can barely see through my watery eyes that it's only a dog after all. Watch, he'll be meaner than Rotter and Aldolf put together. I'll ignore him, and maybe he'll leave me alone. I take a deep breath and look at the ground ahead of me as I trot along. Okay, he's almost in front of me now. I'll keep minding my own business and . . .

"K-10! What on earth happened to you?"

"Pearl? Is that you? I found your message. Is your house near here?"

"It's not far. I couldn't make my family understand that we had to come back for you, so I had to run away."

"You left your family for me?"

Pearl gives me a once-over. "Yes, I did. Hard to believe, now that I see you again. What was I thinking? What is the longest you've ever stayed out of trouble, K-10? About half an hour?"

"Not quite that long." I try to smile, but the quills poke in deeper.

"Hold still," Pearl says. She tries to grip a quill with her teeth. "It's too slippery. We need a human to do this. They have a tool for it."

"Pliers," I say.

"Exactly. Come on. Mr. Rinaldi will know what to do."

"But you ran away," I say. "They'll be mad at you."

"Maybe, but I ran away to find you. Now we're both going home."

She turns, and I follow her. We trot down the road together, almost like old times.

"Do you think your family is out looking for you?" I ask.

"They probably don't know I'm gone. I climbed over the back fence. Never tried that before. Never will again, either."

A few blocks later, Pearl says, "This is it."

We go up a front sidewalk, and she barks at the door. A kid opens it.

"That's Tony," she says.

Tony looks at her, then glances over his shoulder. "What the heck? Weren't you in the backyard?"

Pearl goes inside and I start to follow, but Tony blocks my way with his foot. "Whoa. Wait a minute. Who are you? Hey, Dad, come here!"

Mr. Rinaldi walks in from the next room. "Whose dog is that?"

Tony shrugs. "I don't know. He followed Pearl home, I guess."

"What do you mean, he followed her home? Did she run off again?"

"Yeah. She was on the front steps, barking."

Mr. Rinaldi reaches over to close the door. "Don't let that stray in here."

Pearl runs back out through the opening. "K-10 is my friend. I want him to live here." This time Pearl doesn't rely on barking to get her point across. She stands right next to me, looking up at Mr. Rinaldi.

He tugs on her collar to pull her inside, but she won't budge.

"I think this dog is her friend," Tony says. "Maybe she met him when she was lost. I'm pretty sure I saw him at the campground. He must have tangled with a porcupine."

Mr. Rinaldi leans down and looks at me. "Poor thing sure got a snoutful."

"Can we keep him, Dad?" Tony asks.

"We don't know anything about him, Tony. The people at the campground said a stray was hanging around Pearl. This is probably him. We do have to help him, though. The vets are all closed now, but those quills need to come out right away." He opens the door, and I follow Pearl inside.

"Can he be my dog, Dad?" Tony asks. "I

mean, if he turns out to be okay, and if he doesn't belong to anybody."

"Maybe, Tony. Let's take one thing at a time here."

"Can I take out the quills? We learned how in Scouts."

"It's a painful process, Tony. I can't let you do it, because the dog might bite."

"I don't bite," I say.

"Hush," Pearl says.

"Take him into the family room," Mr. Rinaldi says. Tony leads me into a room with a lot of windows. I can see a yard with a tall wooden fence out back. "Is that what you climbed over?" I ask Pearl. She nods. "Pretty impressive," I say.

Mr. Rinaldi comes back wearing thick leather gloves and carrying pliers. "Come on, boy. Lie down here and let me help you."

This looks pretty scary to me. "Maybe if I just run away, the quills will drop out on their own," I say to Pearl.

Pearl snorts. "Don't be a fool, K-10. Just grit your teeth and let him do this. It'll be over before you know it."

Mr. Rinaldi has me lie on my side on the rug. He grabs one of the quills and pulls. The pain feels like fire. I feel a yip rising up in my throat, but I swallow it and lick my lips.

"Good boy," Mr. Rinaldi says, and pats my head with his big, gloved hand. He has kind eyes.

He pulls out a few more quills. One hurts so much, I want to grab his hand with my teeth and chomp down hard, but I don't. I look up at Pearl.

"I know," she says with a quiet little whine.

Tony has been watching over his dad's shoulder. "Can I do it now, Dad? The dog is good. He's not going to bite me. And if he's going to be my dog, I should be the one taking care of him."

Mr. Rinaldi takes off his gloves. "All right, but wear these."

Tony leans in close to me. "I know this hurts bad, but if you can just hang in there, I'll try to do it as fast as I can, okay?" He's kind of nervous. His scent tells me that.

I give a little woof. "It's okay. You can do it."

I can't help shuddering when Tony pulls out the first quill, but he seems so upset about hurting me, I grit my teeth and try to hold absolutely still after that.

The two younger kids come running in from outside. "Did we get a new dog?" Sam, the youngest, asks. "I want to think up a name for him."

"Tony should name him," the father says. "The dog will belong to him."

Pearl lies down next to me and rests her muzzle on her paws. "Looks like you've won them over. No telling what Tony will come up with for a name, though. Smackers was his bright idea. Of course, he was only a little kid then."

Little Sam sticks his nose practically in my face. "Hey, Tony, what are you doing, huh? What are those pointy things in his snout?"

"You boys go in the other room," Mr. Rinaldi says. "Tony needs quiet to get these quills out. You can see the dog later."

Tony winces every time he pulls out a quill, as if it's hurting him as much as me. I like the way he runs his tongue around his lips while he's concentrating. He pulls the quills out straight and fast, so it doesn't hurt as much as when Mr. Rinaldi did it. I bet Tony could be a vet someday. His scent tells me he's more sure of himself now.

Tony is definitely a dog person. He understands me. I close my eyes and picture the two of us playing ball and going for hikes together. Well, the three of us, because Pearl will be there, too. This is a kid I could hang out with for life. He doesn't remind me of Noah at all. Tony is his own person, and I like him already.

"I wish I knew your name, boy," Tony says. "What is it, anyway?"

"K-10," I say. "You know how most dogs are canines? Get it? Like the number nine?"

Pearl rolls her eyes. "He's not going to get that, K-10. He'll call you something like Rover."

Tony says, "You gotta keep quiet, so I don't hurt you," which puts an end to me trying to explain to him about my name.

The younger kids are peeking in from the

kitchen. "It looks like he has a beard," Sam says. "We could call him Santa Claus."

"He's all prickly," says Joey. "Let's call him Prickles."

"Or Bristly," says Sam.

"Spiky."

"Maybe something like Smackers." I hear Pearl chuckle at that one.

"Crackers."

"Quackers."

"Booger."

I can see Joey and Sam out of the corner of my eye. They're punching each other, laughing at their stupid names.

All this time, Tony keeps quietly pulling out the quills one by one, and I smell blood, but I lie there and let him do it, because I know he's helping me.

At the end Mr. Rinaldi brings in a cloth with a sharp scent. "Dab this alcohol on his wounds, Tony. It will keep them from getting infected."

"This is going to sting," Tony warns me. He pats it all over the places where he pulled out the quills. It burns my eyes and makes my nose feel like it will explode, but I let him do it because I trust him.

The little kids are still running around, calling out dumb names.

"I know a good name for him," Tony says.

"Here it comes—Rover," Pearl says with a sly smile.

Tony stands up. "Fearless."

Joey stops running. "Huh?"

"This dog stayed absolutely still and let me pull out more than thirty quills without a whimper. He's the bravest dog I've ever seen. That's why I'm calling him Fearless."

Pearl snorts, but everybody else agrees that the name suits me. I like it. It's strong. I think my mom would approve. It's an even better name than K-10.

Pearl says, "If you think I'm calling you Fearless, you're crazy."

I'm glad Pearl is back to her old self. Having her all nicey-nice made me uneasy. The best thing about Pearl is that you always know where you stand with her.

Tony is feeding me dog biscuits now, as a reward for being brave. Joey and Sam are petting me. I turn to Pearl. "Rover, indeed," I say. Pearl rolls her eyes but can't hide the slightest hint of a smile. I smile back and settle into the warmth of my new family. I think I'm finally in my forever home—the last home I'll ever need.